Declan (Wounded Heroes #1)
Ava Manello

Published by KBK Publishing
© Ava Manello

ISBN: 978-0-9932436-0-8

Cover Designer: Margreet Asselbergs

ALL RIGHTS RESERVED. This book contains material protected under International and Federal Copyright Laws and Treaties. Any unauthorized reprint or use of this material is prohibited. No part of this book may be reproduced or transmitted in any form or by any means, electronic or mechanical, including photocopying, recording, or by any information storage and retrieval system without express written permission from the author / publisher.

DEDICATION

I thought long and hard about who I should dedicate this book to. I wanted it to be something special and that's why I decided on the following.

I dedicate this book to those who have served or are still serving in the Armed Forces. To those who have given up their lives on the battlefield, or after as a result of the injuries or trauma that they suffered. To those who lost loved ones serving their country.

We owe a massive debt of gratitude to the men and women, who put their lives on the line in order to protect us, to the families who raised them, loved them and gave them up so that they could serve us.

"They shall grow not old, as we that are left grow old: Age shall not weary them, nor the years condemn. At the going down of the sun and in the morning, We will remember them."

Laurence Binyon

WOUNDED HEROES

PROLOGUE

DECLAN

The touch of my fingers sends a small tremor through her. I try to keep the massage firm, yet tender. I can already see some of the tension leaving her body. She groans as I knead the hard knot at the base of her neck. This past week has been a living nightmare for all of us, but especially her and the stress has really knotted her neck and shoulders.

My hands leave her skin for a moment as I reach for more body lotion. She moans in protest. There's a delicate hint of coconut in the air as I warm it in my hands before applying it at the base of her spine.

I knead up and down her back, leaving a trail of warmth where I've passed. I can feel my cock twitching in my tight boxer briefs, begging to be let loose. It's been too long since I allowed myself that particular pleasure. After everything that's happened I wasn't sure it would show interest in sex again, I'm pleased that it is, but I can't. Not here. Not now.

Georgia is laying face down underneath me, dressed only in skimpy briefs so that I can massage her back. My legs are astride hers and I'm pretty sure she can feel my cock pushing against her. She says nothing though.

How the fuck did I find myself here? On this bed and in this position? This is my friend's widow for fucks sake. I need to show him some respect. I need to remember the man that he was, not the shell he had become. He sank so low that there was no coming back. That's why I'm here. We buried him today, so the last place I should be right now is in his widow's bed.

I couldn't ignore Georgia's scream though as she'd woken from a nightmare, or the fat tears rolling down her face. She's too young to be a widow; she's not even forty. She has her whole life ahead of her. I'd consoled her by drawing her into my arms, sitting on the edge of the bed and pulling her close. She'd whimpered when my hand touched her back. The downside of living with Max for these past few months had been the abuse. She may have outgrown most of the bruises but the residual pain was still there.

I'd offered her a back rub in my innocence, and that's how I came to find myself here now, sitting on top of her and desperately begging my cock to go back into its usual state of stupor.

There's something sensuous about caressing a woman's skin, and it's turning me on. As awful as it sounds it helps that I can't see Georgia's face. I couldn't do this if I looked her in the eye. I need to just pretend she's some anonymous stranger if I've any chance of getting through the rest of this night.

Georgia moans as I release a particularly deep knot in her shoulder, but it sounds more like a moan of passion than relief.

"Declan," she pleads. "I need you. I need this." She whimpers.
"I can't." I whisper back. "I can't do it to Max." I apologise.

"Fuck Max." She hisses. "He didn't give a shit about either of us these past few months. I need this." She pauses. "And from the feel of your cock digging into my ass you need it too." She reasons.

She's right. I do need it. But I can't.

"I can't look you in the eye." I apologise.

"Then don't." She reasons. She reaches down behind her, pulling her almost non-existent underwear down and raising her ass slightly. I can see her glistening pussy. She's wet for me and I know for sure that my cock is hard for her.

I dismiss the guilt from my mind and release myself from my boxer shorts. Without allowing myself time to think about it I push into her. Fuck! That feels so good. It feels so tight and deep. I pause for a moment just enjoying the sensation, and Georgia lets out a loud groan of satisfaction.

"That feels fucking amazing." She almost purrs.

Slowly I move in and out of her, each time it feels like I've gone deeper than the last. Her legs are trapped together between mine by her shoved down underwear and her ass is gripping tightly to my cock as I move in and out.

She moves a hand to caress my leg. I stop her by holding her arms down. From the satisfied moans she's making, it's clear she likes that. Her face is almost hidden in the mattress, the pillow already tossed aside. She's got short hair, I want to grab hold of it and pull her head back each time I push into her, but it's too short for that. It's just long enough to hide her face, and that's probably a good thing. If I saw her face right now I suspect my cock would deflate faster than a popped balloon.

The only sounds in the room are the slap of flesh against flesh as my movements become stronger as do our mutual groans of pleasure. I slap her ass sharply, and when she doesn't protest I do it again. She's pushing her ass back up against me, silently begging for more. I give it to her.

That's when it all goes to shit. I'm having the best sex I've had in months, fuck it I'm having the only sex I've had in months, when I hear it.

A car backfires outside and I lose it. Suddenly I'm not in this suburban bedroom; I'm back in Afghanistan the day it happened. I can feel the heat, taste the sand in my mouth, and hear the screams of the other guys.

I snap out of it, just in time. My hands are round Georgia's neck and I'm strangling her. She can barely breathe, let alone make a sound and her face is going a shade of purple. I release my hands quickly.

Georgia draws in a deep gulping breath of air before collapsing back down to the mattress and taking shallow breaths.

"What the fuck!" She croaks, her voice barely there and raspy.

What do I say; how the fuck do I explain the nightmare that I live constantly? I can't. Instead I do the most dick move possible. I pull out of her and rush from the room without explanation.

Within minutes my bag is packed and I'm gone. Driving to an unknown destination in the dark of the night. I didn't even say I was sorry.

I'm not sure where to go so I just drive. I'm not fit to be around normal people. Something broke in me out in Afghanistan, and I'm not sure I can ever be mended.

So I drive, and wait to see where the road takes me.

CHAPTER ONE

DECLAN - THREE MONTHS EARLIER

The sand is so fine it's like dust, invading everywhere regardless of how well you pack your kit away. Afghanistan may have some beautiful scenery, but right now it's my idea of hell. The cold nights make way to blistering days, the sun scorching the parched earth, and dehydrating you faster than you can take fluids on board. Even here in the supposed shelter of the tent I can still taste it.

This place is supposed to be our sanctuary, our respite from the day's challenges, yet it feels more and more like a prison. Armed soldiers patrol the high fence, the sniper tower is constantly on alert and yet we pretend that on this side of the fence we are home. We couldn't be further away if we tried, here in a country where I'm not even sure we belong. The residents don't want us, the Taliban sure as shit don't want us and our families back home can't understand why we're here fighting someone else's war.

I've long since stopped trying to make sense of it. Just joining the Army cost me my girlfriend; she couldn't understand why I didn't want to stay and set up home with her in Australia. I couldn't explain it. It's like a deep seated need in me to be part of this. Or it used to be. Now after so many years of service, of seeing friends blown up or shot, of attending funeral after funeral, I've become immune. I've forgotten why I wanted to sign up. I just want this to be over and to go home. There's nothing for me at home, but right now, anywhere is better than here.

I'm a Corporal in the SASR (Australian Special Air Service Regiment) and as part of 4 Squadron; I lead a patrol of five guys. We've almost reached the end of our six-month rotation out here, and we're all looking forward to this one finishing. This will be the last tour for most of us. That means going back to civilian life. We've become so dependent on each other out here, it's going to be strange not living out of each other's pockets back home.

We can communicate without saying a word; so finely tuned to each other that a look or a nod of the head often suffices. We've bonded and become brothers over the last few years. This is the life we know. Fuck, it's the only life I know. Going back to normal feels more alien to me than anything I've experienced so far.

We've all come from coastal towns on the west side of Australia so this constant desert sand makes us miss the coast even more. I miss the kiss of the breeze in the air, the tang of the salt from the ocean on my tongue. Shit. I've got to pull myself out of this mood. I can't afford to become melancholy out here. Lives depend on me. I have to be alert at all times.

There's a ruckus outside the tent that tells me the guys are back from the cookhouse. Cameron is taking the piss out of Max yet again for wanting to re-enlist at the end of the tour. The rest of us can't wait to get home and as far away from this hellhole as possible. I don't understand Max. He's married, happily last I heard, which is unusual for guys like us and I know he and Georgia were talking about starting a family when he goes home at the end of this rotation.

We all enlisted at the same time, and have gone through training together as well as a shit load of deployments into situations you wouldn't wish on your worst enemy. We've been taught to kill stealthily and silently, to go in and rescue hostages, how to blow shit up and just be a general bad ass. There must be something missing in each of us because we used to love this shit. What normal person gets off on this kind of life? The key words there though are 'used to'. It's become a taboo subject none of us dare mention. What's changed to make us feel this way?

Over the last couple of years there've been an increasing number of green on black attacks. The people we're here to teach to protect their own country are turning on us, killing us, and it's no longer black and white. The only guys I trust anymore are my own unit. None of us can sleep safe in our beds anymore. It got a little too close to home last year when one of our colleagues was shot while playing football with some of the local soldiers. One of the guys on his own fucking team just casually reached into his trousers, pulled a gun out and shot Glen point blank. His own team!

I try and pull myself together before the team sees me. They don't need my negative mood to bring them down as well. I look up with a smile on my face, as Cameron is the first into the tent. He's a good-looking bastard, short dark hair, tanned complexion and dark eyes. Whenever we go out he's always the first to pull. He's probably the closest thing I've got to a brother. We keep talking about setting up in some sort of business when we get out of here.

Max closely follows him. He's the odd one out, the only one that's married and yet the only one who doesn't want to go home. He's a little older than the rest of us, in his early thirties and we often call him Grandpa to tease him. He's probably the most calming influence on the group; I think he'll make a great

Dad, as he's great at handling our petty conflicts or offering advice. I'll miss him when he doesn't come back with us.

Luke is the quiet one. He keeps his dark hair closely shaved and his brown eyes look like he holds the secrets to the universe. He watches and listens, and for all that he's so quiet he's the most deadly of us. He can take a sniper shot better than any of us. They always say it's the quiet ones you have to watch out for.

Ryan's the joker of the group. Even in this heat he wears that bloody beanie hat when we're off duty, along with his full dark sunglasses. He'd like to think he's dark and mysterious, but with his short blonde hair and cheeky grin he's the cutest of us as well. He gets nearly as many women as Cameron.

Jacko, or Jacob as he's formally known, is the serious one. He's a vet, or he will be when he takes his final exams. He'd almost qualified when he shocked the shit out of his parents by enlisting. It happened just days after his best friend from high school was killed out here. His parents begged him not to, but like the rest of us, it was some kind of calling that he couldn't ignore. He's the messiest in our unit, from his scruffy tousled hair to the stubble on his chin. For all that, he keeps his kit immaculate. We all do. We rely on it to keep us alive.

We all grew up around Perth in outlying suburbs, but it's a vast area meaning that none of us had met before basic training.

We quickly bonded, we're so tight together when we're working, but somehow seem to drift apart when we get home. It never lasts long as we can't go over a month without all meeting up and hitting a bar or two.

The last few visits home have affected us all. The more we struggle with being out here the more we're finding our loved ones struggling with it as well. It's gone on too long, there's been too much blood shed and there seems to be no end in sight. Not to mention all of our families think its someone else's war, and that we shouldn't be out here. We're starting to agree with them.

Don't get me wrong. It's not all hell out here. Not everyone we meet wants to shoot us where we stand. The scenery is beautiful and some of the locals are the kindest, most gracious people I've come across. They're happy in their poverty because they don't aspire to anything else. Fuck, back home everyone wants the biggest TV, a better house than his or her neighbour or the fastest car. It's all shit. Its just stuff. Stuff that in the grand scheme of things means nothing. These people have nothing so don't know any better. They're fighting every day to survive, and yet they're happy and gracious with it. It's greed that brought us to this hellhole in the first place. One man wanted more than he was given and that's what starts wars. Greed. Some despot decides that they're entitled to more and instead of earning it, they take it. Then idiots like our unit are sent in to make it right. What happens is that idiots like us die for someone else's argument.

I've got to shake myself out of this maudlin mood. It won't shift. It's been like a black cloud over my head for the past week at least. The closer it comes to ending our deployment and going home, the more unnecessary our time here feels.

There's a shout from outside the tent. "Yo, Declan!" shouts my Captain. "It's time."

The guys don't wait for my command; we've done this so often the routine comes naturally. Within moments they're packed up and we're all heading out to our Nary patrol vehicle. M4 carbines slung over our shoulders and Glock's holstered in our belts. The heavy protective equipment is dragging us down in the 130 degree heat, but none of us will go out without it.

The Nary is our armoured beast. It looks like something I built out of Meccano as a child, all chunky, square and sand coloured. It's open topped to give us mobility with the guns and grenade launcher, but its armour is supposed to protect us from stray bullets and IED devices, those sneaky little devices that are hidden in the ground and designed to blow a man to shreds. I've buried more than one friend thanks to those bastards. It's fast on this terrain, which is what we need, and it can handle the gullies and rutted roads we have to work along. It's also the ugliest vehicle I've ever seen. I swear when I get home I'm getting my bike out of storage and going back onto two wheels.

I take my command seat in the front of the vehicle and signal for Cameron to head us out for todays patrol. It's one patrol closer to going home.

CHAPTER TWO

DECLAN

The patrol so far has been boring and routine. I'm no longer sure why we're doing this, other than a guy behind a desk in Perth thinks we should. From what I've heard it's not going to be much longer before all the Australian forces are pulled out of here. Right now that day can't come soon enough.

A small child runs out onto the rough road in front of us, and I signal to Cameron to stop. It looks like he's innocently chasing a ball that's gone astray from the soccer game on the rough ground to the left of us, but we're trained that in this country nothing is innocent. The children are so immune to the sight of armed soldiers that they don't even flinch when they come into contact with us. This little boy can't be more than six or seven. He stands there in is his tattered robe and bare feet just watching us. There's no fear on his face. He shouldn't have anything to fear from us, but who knows If we have anything to fear from him.

Luke is manning the grenade launcher and on constant alert, as is Ryan who's on the machine gun. They're quiet and taking in our surroundings. Max meanwhile has started whinging, an annoying trait of his lately.

"Just get moving Cameron, let's run the little shit over and get the hell back from this patrol." He mutters. He's losing the ability to see the humanity out here. He no longer sees them as people, but targets. I've had words with him on a few occasions about it, but if it continues I'm going to have to go to the Captain with my concerns. If he doesn't snap out of this mentality he's going to do something stupid, and stupid gets you killed out here.

"Shut up, Max." Cameron doesn't take any notice of Max's glare. He simply remains alert, waiting for the child to pick up the soccer ball and make his way back off the road. As soon as he's clear Cameron sets off again.

I still can't get my head around the fact that a six-year-old child can be a threat. That just doesn't happen where I come from, but out here it's real. The terrorists use women and children as shields, as walking suicide bombs and as soldiers. At home kids his age are in school learning English and Maths. Out here they're learning how to work a Kalashnikov and how to shoot to kill.

Max finally stops his muttering once we're clear of the soccer game. There's no conversation as we patrol, we're all too alert to our surroundings, watching for the glint of a sniper rifle or any hint of rebel activity.

We're on the return leg of the patrol when it all goes to shit. We've visited the outlying post, dropped off some medical supplies, swapped Intel and are in sight of the base when it happens.

There's some obstacle in the road ahead of us, it looks like a dirty bundle of clothes, and Cameron moves over to the side of the road to get past it. I'm about to tell him to stop the Nary when he hits the IED with the front wheel.

The majority of casualties in this war have been caused by IED's. That's an improvised explosive device or roadside bomb. They're hidden on the routes that we commonly travel and are designed to blow us to kingdom come. We're always on the lookout for them, but even if we've swept the route one day they can be there the next as they're hidden under cover of darkness.

The Nary is heavily armoured against IED's, but its still no match for this one. The angle and force of the explosion throw the vehicle into the air and it tips over. What you've got to remember is that although this feels like it's playing out in slow motion, it's happening fast. It's a split second from the wheel hitting the device to us finding ourselves arse over tit on the road. There's an acrid smell that could be burning rubber, and my ears are ringing from the force of the blast. Everything's muffled and I can't hear Cameron although I can see his mouth is moving.

I try and turn my head to see where Luke and Jacko are, but something's pinning me down. There's dust everywhere and I can't see for shit right now. My hearing starts to return at around the same time my head feels like it's going to explode. I think I can feel my fingers and toes so I'm guessing I've just got a concussion.

Just before I pass out I swear I can hear Max screaming about saving his leg.

CHAPTER THREE

DECLAN

I wake in the middle of the night, yet another nightmare yanking me from a restless sleep. Throwing the covers from the bed as I can't stand the feeling of confinement. It takes me back to the day the IED went off. We were so fucking lucky that day. We all walked away with our lives, well most of us did. Max was sent home on a medical evacuation. He almost lost his leg that day. His army career is over. It's a bitter irony that out of all of us he's the only one who wanted to be there, and now he's the only one who can't go back.

Despite doing a dangerous job every day your own mortality isn't something you ever really think about. Sure, we have to write our death letters before we embark on a mission, just in case we don't come home, and we all have our photo taken just in case the press needs an image to go along with an obituary, but you don't think about it. If you did you'd never get out of bed on a morning. The letter and photo are just part of getting ready to go to work, the same way we make sure our kit is all present and correct, our gun is cleaned and we have plenty of ammunition.

It took over two hours to release Max from the wreckage. The last hour was the scariest as that's when he stopped screaming. In my whole life I've never heard anything worse than that silence. I thought we'd lost him. We all did. The medics kept trying to get the rest of us back to the base hospital, but you don't leave a man behind. That's not our code.

I'd been the first out of the crashed vehicle. It was sheer gut instinct that caused me to turn. I looked into the eyes of the terrorist who'd been creeping up on us, knife at the ready to slit our throats. I continued looking into his eyes as I put a bullet between them. The guys keep telling me I'm a hero, that I saved all our lives that day. I'm not a fucking hero, I just reacted the way I've been trained to. It was as natural as breathing, and nothing that any of them wouldn't have done in my place.

Max is due out of the hospital later today, Georgia has been keeping us updated on his progress, but he refused to let us visit. We're all heading over to his house to welcome him home, although she's warned us he's changed. He's not the guy we remember. I'm sure that once he's home it will make things better, no one likes being cooped up in a hospital after all. That said, I'm home and things aren't better. I'm suffering nightmares; that's when I can sleep. I'm jumping every time I hear a loud noise, constantly on alert and suspicious of everyone around me. The army want me to see a shrink, but I'm fighting it. There's nothing wrong with me. I just need time.

Everyone is dealing with this in his own way. Normally we'd have been meeting up regularly, laughing and joking over a beer or two or three. Today's going to be the first time we've seen each other since we got home. It's as though none of us can face each other. I can't face the guys. I feel as though I let them down. As the Sergeant it was my job to keep everyone safe and I failed. Max almost lost his life, never mind his leg. He's not out of the woods yet, the surgeons are still muttering about taking it off at the ankle, as it's not healing properly.

I've been hiding out at the apartment I live in above my grandmother's barn. It's basic, it's secluded and it's peaceful. My gran understands somehow. Aside from hugging the life out of me when I came home, she's not mentioned it. She just told me that she was here for me when I was ready to talk about it, then walked off to cook dinner.

How the fuck can I talk about what I've seen, what I've done to my ninety year old Gran? She wouldn't understand. Shit, I don't understand it. I joined the army to do good, to do something I could be proud of. I'm not proud of my time in Afghanistan. Fuck. That terrorist I killed that day was barely a teen. I killed a child. No matter how often I try and justify it, tell myself he would have killed us all without a second thought, it doesn't help. It's why I can't be around people right now. Everywhere I turn there are families with kids, kids no older than he was. I can't escape it. I can't stop re-living that day.

Sleep is being elusive so I reach for the bottle of Jack Daniel's at the side of the bed and take a long shot. It's no good. There's no welcome burn as it hits my throat. It's no more effective than a can of soda; I've become immune to its effect since I came home. The bottle's empty so I toss it aside, groaning as I hear the clink of glass as it hit's the pile of empties already on the floor.

Rising slowly from the bed I catch sight of my reflection in the early dawn light. It's not flattering. I've not shaved since I came home and I'm not sure I can remember the last time I had a shower, it certainly wasn't this week that's for sure.

Gran gave up on me sometime last week, tired of taking back plates of congealed and untouched food. She muttered some curse at me as she went. She knows me well enough to leave me be right now.

My clothes stink. They haven't been changed since my last shower either. They're crumpled and smell of sweat and booze. I look like a fucking hobo that's for sure.

I drag myself into the bathroom and switch on the shower. I can't let my men see me like this; they need me to be the strong one. As I step under the warm stream and feel the dirt and grime burn away from my skin I'm left wondering how the hell I'm supposed to become the man I used to be again.

CHAPTER FOUR

DECLAN

Turns out that Gran hadn't given up on me; she was just biding her time. As soon as I stepped out of the shower she was waiting. I'm glad I wrapped a towel round me before I left the bathroom.

My Gran is the sort of old lady who doesn't have to speak. You can tell exactly what she's thinking from the way she looks at you. Her current look is telling me that I've fucked up.

"Get yourself dressed and come over for coffee." She instructs. I don't miss the drawn in breath as she surveys the wreckage of the room on her way out. This could go one of two ways. Either she'll offer me some advice that I'll accept or she'll send me packing. Right now I'm not sure which option I'd prefer.

The sun is bright and hurts my eyes after the gloom of my room. I shield my eyes as I hurry across the yard to the kitchen door. I love the smell of Gran's kitchen. It's a homely, comforting smell. Many a morning in Afghanistan I wanted to be sat here at the table with her, sampling her scones and listening to tales of the old days.

My Gran is a strong woman; she's had to be. She lost my Granddad, the love of her life, when he was only 42. He had a heart attack out on the back field; by the time anyone realized he was missing it was too late. Since then she's raised my Mum and Uncle and then me on her own. She has farm hands these days, but that's no excuse for my not helping out since I came home. I should have been more concerned with how she was getting on rather than wallowing in my own misery.

Gran points to the table when I walk in. There's already a steaming black coffee waiting for me along with one of her scones, freshly baked and oozing with butter. I devour it like a starving man which earns a tut of disapproval.

"Sorry, Gran." I offer with my mouth still full. "These are good. Any chance of another one?" I grin at her. My cheeky grin softens the sour expression on her face and she pats my shoulder affectionately as she walks past me to the counter.

"What's happened to you Declan?" She asks. I don't want to have this conversation with her, not now, not today. If I'm honest I don't want to have this conversation any time.

"I don't know, Gran." I offer weakly. "I just feel out of place, like I've failed some test or something. Like I don't belong anywhere." It sounds feeble. I can't put how I'm feeling into words. It was never my strong point to start with, and that's only got worse since I came back.

"You've given up on life." She states as she sits down opposite me again, passing me another huge scone. "I never thought I'd see that from you, you're stronger than that." It's a statement. She's not asking me, she's telling me.
"I'm not as strong as you, Gran."

"Stuff and bloody nonsense. You're your Granddads' flesh and blood and mine. That's a strong mix, Declan. You just need to get your head out of your ass and get on with living." I almost spit my coffee out when I hear Gran using the word ass. It's not in her normal vocabulary. She's normally so well spoken.

"Your Granddad was making plans for tomorrow the day he died." She carries on. "None of us knew he wouldn't get one. Life is too short to be wasted, you've got to get up and live it." She pauses, looking reflectful. I can only guess she's thinking of my Granddad.

"I'm not wasting my life." I protest.

"You've not left that room in a week, Declan. You've quit on yourself. What's that if it's not wasting your life?"

I don't have an answer for her. She's right.

"What do you want to do with your life now you're out of the Army?" She questions.

"I thought I'd help you with the farm." I offer. Gran shakes her head.

"You're not hiding away here with me young man. I've got more than enough help from my farm hands. You've got a week to do some serious thinking, then we're going to sit down again and you're going to tell me what you're going to do with the rest of your life." She stands abruptly, pausing just long enough to place a gentle kiss on my forehead before she leaves the room.

My Gran doesn't take any crap from anyone. She may look frail, but she's a pretty formidable lady. If she says I have a week then I'd best get on with it and work out what I'm going to do with my future. She's right. I can't continue to hide away on the farm like I have.

The only problem is I don't have a clue what I'm going to do.

CHAPTER FIVE

DECLAN

I'm nearly in the city when the phone rings. I almost ignore it but see Georgia's name on the display so hit the hands free button.

"Hey, Georgia. How's our guy?" I try to sound cheerful for her sake.

"Not good, Declan. That's why I'm calling." She sounds like she's about to break into tears. "I let slip you guys were coming over when we get home and he went off on one." She pauses and I'm sure I hear her holding back a sob. This is the side we never think about when we're on tour. The family back home, and how it affects them. I guess we have to be fairly selfish to do the job we do. It's only now that one of us has been seriously injured that I'm seeing it.

"He... he said you can't come round." It's obvious she's embarrassed telling me this.

"It's okay, we'll give him some time, let him settle in." I offer. "Just let us know how he's doing and we'll sort out another time to come see him."

"You sure?" She sounds so relieved. I can't imagine the pressure she's been under. Max isn't the easiest guy to get on with when he's fit and well, I can't imagine what it's like for her now he's incapacitated.

"Course. I'll let the guys know. I'm almost in the city now anyway so I'll just meet up for a drink with them instead."

"Thanks, Declan." Her voice is a little calmer now that the pressure of our visit is off the horizon.

"Promise you'll let me know if you need anything?" I tell her.

"I promise, and thank you Declan." Before I can reply the phone has gone dead.

Part of me is pissed off at the wasted journey, but I suppose it gives me chance to restock the booze cupboard if nothing else. I'm not sure I'm happy about meeting up with the guys, which is scary. They're like brothers to me. I just can't face them truth be told.

For fucks sake, I'm in the SAS, I can face terrorists, war zones, and a gun in my face. I need to man the fuck up here and get on with it. It's probably going to be like most things in life, a damn site easier than you anticipate. All too often we build up scenarios in our head, make them into some big thing that stop us doing things or moving forward out of fear, when in reality there's nothing to be worried about at all.

I hit the speed dial on the phone for Cameron. He can tell the rest of the guys. The whole conversation I find myself second-guessing him, is that a different tone I hear in his voice? Is he really as pleased to hear from me as he sounds? I'm imagining things that aren't there I'm sure. Fuck, I'm seeing things that aren't there and hearing things that don't exist all the time. Every corner I turn, every shadow I see out of the corner of my eye takes me back there.

I can finally see the sea ahead of me. I've got an hour before we've arranged to meet up. I prescribe myself some time on the beach, maybe if I walk through the surf it will help remind me that I'm back home, away from that hell hole.

I indicate to move into the lane for the coastal road, winding the window down and turning the air con off. I can taste the tang of the salt from the ocean. I am home, I can feel it, I just wish my brain would accept it.

CHAPTER SIX

DECLAN

The walk on the beach was just what I needed. I've stopped second guessing the conversation with Cameron and tried thinking about what my Gran said this morning. I'm no closer to a solution other than knowing she's right. I've got to start living again.

The bar is crowded and noisy when I arrive, most of the noise coming from a table in the far corner. As I suspect that's the table full of my guys. As nervous as I was about meeting them a huge grin breaks out on my face when I see them. Cameron stands when he sees me, shouting and gesturing me over to their table. As if I'd have missed them with the noise they're making. They all seem to be in good spirits, no one gives me any indication that our friendship has changed in any way, just the opposite. I'm greeted as warmly as ever. Cameron even tells me how much he's missed me.

Looking at the guys you can't tell that just a short time ago we were all in a war zone, trapped in a vehicle that had been blown up. They all look carefree and untroubled. I don't understand why they look so normal and I feel so far from it.

Jacko is moaning about having to enrol back in college to complete his veterinary training. He's found a job as an assistant at a practice in Perth and they're sponsoring him becoming qualified. He's also found a hot vet nurse that he's spending a lot of time with from the sounds of it.

Cameron is on a self confessed holiday. Like me he doesn't know what he wants to do, he just wants to kick back for a few months and see what takes his fancy.

Luke is still the silent, brooding one. With his sniper skills I wouldn't be surprised if he signed up for private security work, but when Cameron suggests it he quickly shoots the idea down.

"I've had enough of that life for now. I think I may go into property renovation instead." He tells us. That surprises us all, but then he has always been a pretty good handyman, always fixing the broken kit and equipment without complaint. He goes onto explain that he's been saving his cash and found a property he'd like to buy and renovate. He can do most of the work himself, and just hire in the trades as he needs them.

"Sounds good." Cameron smiles. "Me and Declan can help you if you want?" The bloody git has a habit of volunteering me for things without asking, yet I don't correct him. A bit of good, hard manual labour might be just what I need right now. At least if I'm busy grafting I won't have time to think and sink back into that dark place I've been in.

Conversation turns to Max. None of us has been able to see him since we got back from Afghanistan. He's found excuse after excuse to keep us away. I know that he's still at risk of losing his leg, and that his hope of going back for another tour have been dashed, but I'm surprised at the way he's keeping us all at arms length.

"I'll give him a couple of days to settle in at home, then I'm going round there, invited or not." I tell the guys.

"Do you want me to come with you?" Cameron offers.

"Not this time. Let me see how the land lies first. I don't want to scare him off." I suggest. I don't know what's wrong with Max, but I do sense that I have to handle him carefully. Fuck – I've come home messed up to shit mentally and I haven't got the injuries that he's got.

We spend the rest of the afternoon drinking, reminiscing and singing. By the time we're kicked out at closing none of us can walk in a straight line so we all head back to Cameron's and crash on his floor.

For an afternoon I've managed to forget my fears and worries thanks to good friends and alcohol, but I've got to be careful, I can't use alcohol as a crutch any longer. I know I need help, but I'm not sure that I'm strong enough to ask for it.

For the first time in my life I feel weak.

CHAPTER SEVEN

DECLAN

I've given Max the week I promised, it seems fitting somehow as it's the same week that Gran has allowed me. I've spent a lot of time thinking about what I want to do and am no wiser, so Cam and I are going to go help Luke work on his renovation project. I figure some good hard labour will do me good. I've tried to help out on the farm this week, but I'm surplus to requirements. They farm hands have a routine and they like to stick to it. There's not even any maintenance for me to do, Gran runs a tight ship. She seems happy though that at least I have an interim plan, something to keep me busy and stop me brooding as she calls it.

I've spent most of the week tinkering with my bike, changing the oil, checking the battery charge level, the electrics and making sure there's enough air in the tyres. It's not got enough mileage on it yet to have any concerns. I've barely put 1000 kilometres on it since I brought it home from the showroom.

It's a Triumph Tiger XC SE 800, built a little like the Nary in that it can handle off road with ease, but a damn sight better looking and a lot more fun. I've decided to take the bike today, it's only an hour to where Max lives in Rockingham from here, at least it is the way I ride and I've missed the feel of being out there on two wheels.

The ride passes by too quickly; I've missed being out on the bike. Max lives near the shopping centre rather than on the coast road. They bought this place because it was close to a good school and they were thinking ahead. It's a little too suburban after Harvey. Then again coming from a place with only just over 5000 residents to one that's twenty times bigger will always be a bit too much for me. I bring the bike to a stop under the carport and pull of my helmet. I can hear the muffled sounds of an argument coming from in the house. Great. Just what I needed to walk into.

"Whoever it is tell them to fuck off." Max's voice rises above the buzz of the air con extractor, clearly audible through the solid wood front door. I ring the bell anyway.

The click of heels on the tiled hallway lets me know that it's probably Georgia who's coming to greet me. I'm a little shocked when she opens the door; she looks to have aged years since I last saw her. Her short hair looks lank and unbrushed, which is something I've never seen. Georgia always has been shit hot about taking care of her appearance. She has dark circles under her eyes, and if I'm not mistaken the shadow of a bruise around her eye which she's tried to disguise with makeup.

"Hi, Declan." There's little warmth in her greeting. She pauses to check over her shoulder. "It's not a good time right now." She explains apologetically.

"I said tell them to fuck off." Max shouts again from the lounge. Georgia draws in a breath as though to steel herself.

"But it's Declan." She answers back cheerfully. "Surely you want to see him?" She sounds defeated. I don't give Max chance to answer as I gently push Georgia aside and head into the lounge.

Max, to put it simply, looks like shit. He's unshaven, there are food stains on his t-shirt that is hanging too loose on him, and you can barely see his leg for the metal framework full of screws that are holding it together. The wounds around the screws look red and angry and his leg is grey against the coffee table that he has it propped up on. He gives me a dirty look as I get closer.

"I said fuck off. I don't want visitors." Max mutters, taking another mouthful from the neck of the bottle of whisky clutched in his hand. It's only ten am and he's already three sheets to the wind. I look around for Georgia expecting her to have followed me into the room, but there's no sign of her.

"Well I'm here now so I might as well stay." I grin at Max. It's not returned. Instead I receive a steely and very unfriendly glare. It's like I'm looking into the eyes of a stranger. I know Max can be a moody bugger, but this is different. I know I'm hardly one to say anything as I was in my own whisky stupor last week, but this isn't good. "I'll go round up some coffee for us." I offer, heading off to the kitchen. I've been here enough times to know the layout of the place. As I pass the study I see it's been converted to a makeshift bedroom, knowing Max as I do he'll hate that.

Georgia is sitting at the kitchen worktop, her head in her hands and crying silent tears. She flinches when I put my hand on her arm to get her attention. Confused I lift the arm of her t-shirt a little to find a livid purple bruise in the shape of a hand.

"Don't judge him." She whispers. "He's just having a hard time." She pleads. I ball my hands into fists at the sight of the bruises.

"I don't care how fucking hard a time he's having." I growl. "That doesn't give him the right to hurt you. Why didn't you tell me?" I obviously raise my voice a little too much as she flinches back from me. "I'm sorry, Georgia, but I thought we were friends. You should have called me." I want to pull her into my arms and comfort her, but the way she's holding herself tells me that wouldn't be a good idea. I suspect the bruises on her arms aren't the only ones.

She moves slowly, and I can now see painfully, across the kitchen to fill the coffee maker. Gently I take it from her, gesturing for her to return to her seat at the counter. Whilst I'm prepping the coffee I ask her what the hell's been happening.

"He's in so much pain, the pain meds aren't helping, and they're still not sure he'll be able to keep his leg." Her shoulders sag even further. "We're going to have to sell the house, they've told him even if he does keep his leg he'll never be able to handle the stairs properly and he refuses to get a stair lift." She looks around the kitchen. This house was her pride and joy, her dream home. Now she's going to lose it.

"Surely there's something they can do?" Even as I say the words, I know there obviously isn't. The Army has the best doctors, if they say it can't be fixed, then it can't.

"He's got an appointment with the surgeon tomorrow, they're making the decision then, but it's not looking good. It's not healing properly." She's wringing a washcloth in her hands and it's almost in shreds from the way that she's worrying at it.

"What can I do?" I offer. "What can the guys do?"

"There's nothing you can do." She replies helplessly. "You can't go back and undo that day. You can't give him his job back." She pauses as she draws in another sob. "He says he wishes he was dead."

How can I judge my friend? I was in a bad place last week and had none of the troubles that he has. I was so lost in a bottle I barely knew what day of the week it was. Part of me is angry though; he has Georgia. He has a wife who loves him. That hasn't changed. He needs to be there for her as well. I guess that's part of Army life though, we become selfish, leaving those we love behind for months at a time and only focussing on us, our survival for that time. If we didn't we wouldn't make it through the tour. You can't just switch that off when you come home. I wish we could.

The coffee brewed I leave a mug in front of Georgia and make my way back into the lounge. Max looks at me in disgust when I pass him the coffee, but he takes it anyway, reaching into his pocket and pulling out a coloured pill that he swallows with a mouthful of the hot drink.

"What's that?" I ask, curious, as it doesn't look like any of the pain meds I'm used to seeing.

"None of your fucking business." He grunts in reply. I give him a sharp look. Max has never spoken to me like that before. Discipline is drilled into us, and no matter how angry, you never speak to a commanding officer in that tone.

"Don't look at me like that, we're not in the fucking Army anymore." He tells me petulantly.

"I don't give a shit, Max. What the fuck is up with you? Why are you hitting Georgia?" I raise an eyebrow at him.

"I didn't invite you here, I don't want you here, and what I do or don't do is none of your fucking business anymore, Declan. So finish your coffee and fuck off. You're not wanted here."

I've seen enough for today, staying here isn't going to help anything so I return to the kitchen where I tell Georgia goodbye, and make her promise to call me if she needs me. She nods her head in agreement, but I know it's a false promise.

I need to call Cam and the guys and find out what we can do to help Max. I don't know where to start, I can barely help myself, but I've got to do something. He's our brother, and you never leave a man behind.

CHAPTER EIGHT

DECLAN

The whole ride home to Harvey I kept second-guessing myself. Is there anything that I could have said or done to help Max. Was leaving the right thing to do?

I need to ring my Captain and see if I can call on some psych support at least for him, knowing Max he'll refuse it point blank like I did. There's got to be something we can do.

I call Cameron when we get in; when I mention the tablet he asks me what it looked like. I try and recall it. I think it was a chalky, aqua blue looking tablet with some sort of pattern engraved on it.

"Shit, sounds like he's on Amphetamines." Cameron groans.

"Come off it. You know Max, he's as anti drugs as the rest of us." I offer. We've seen too many friends fall prey to drugs to overcome the stress of combat. "Max is stronger than that."

"Everything you've told me says its drugs, Declan. I know you don't want to believe it. The mood swings, the depression, the anger. They're all classic signs. We need to find out how he's getting them, but you can't just stop him cold turkey, we don't know how long he's been on them."

"I guess I can talk to his Doctor." My response sounds lame even to me. "What do we do? We can't let Georgia go through this on her own."

"Other than helping Luke out with his renovation I've got nothing on, we could stay with him, take it in shifts I guess." Cameron suggests. Knowing Max that's not going to go down well. He's a strong willed individual when he's not messed up on drugs. This isn't going to be easy.

"I'll give Georgia a call, see if we can set it up." It's not going to be easy, but we have to pull together to try and help Max. It's the least we can do. "Does Luke need anymore help?" It wouldn't hurt me to get my hands dirty for a while, right now I really need a distraction, something that will tire me out, help me sleep at night. Sleep hasn't been my friend of late that's for sure.

"I reckon we could do with a hand. He's gutting the whole interior of the house first, then when he's remodelled the garden will need landscaping. Pretty sure he could use a lackey like you." I can hear the smirk in Cameron's voice.

"Cheeky bastard." I laugh. "Just remember who your commanding officer is." I remind him. We chat for the next half hour catching up on who is doing what, and who is doing who, although we've not been able to find out any more about Jacob's mysterious vet nurse since we last met. He's keeping pretty tight lipped on the subject that's for sure.

We end the call with me agreeing to call Georgia and the Captain to see what support we can offer, and what support the Army can offer. Max may be stubborn, but even he can't take on all of us. At least I hope he can't.

CHAPTER NINE

DECLAN

The call I had been putting off all morning is irrelevant now. Georgia just called. The surgeon has made the decision that they need to take Max's leg off mid calf. It's infected, and if they don't deal with it now, he could end up losing it above the knee.

"How long has he been on the drugs?" I ask her.

"How... I don't... how did you know?" she asks guiltily.

"He took them in front of me." I reply, my voice heavy with disgust. "How the fuck did he get hold of them if he couldn't even walk?"

Georgia tells me that she thinks it was one of the other patients in the hospital that started him off, and that a guy has been coming to the house most days. That's why she's covered in bruises, she'd begged Max to stop and he'd lashed out at her.

He's going back into the hospital and Georgia has agreed to let the Doctors know so they can make sure he can't get any more supplies whilst he's in there. It will complicate his recovery, but hopefully he's not too far into the addiction.

SEVERAL HOURS LATER

The phone is ringing and it drags me from yet another nightmare. I grope blindly on the nightstand for it and only succeed in knocking it to the floor. I curse as it continues ringing and vibrating across the floor.

I can't get to it in time and it stops ringing. I've just decided I can't be bothered to leave the comfort of my bed and it can stay there till morning when it starts ringing again.

"Have you seen the fucking time?" I question as I answer it without checking the caller display.

"Declan?" I don't recognise the voice on the other end, other than it's female and it's crying. "He's gone Declan." Through the sobs I realise it's Georgia on the phone.

"What do you mean he's gone?" I'm half awake and can't understand her. The clock says three am. I'm pretty sure the hospital wouldn't have picked him up this early.

"He took an overdose, he left me the fucking coward." She's sobbing loudly now. I shake myself awake trying to understand what she just said.

"What do you mean he left you?" I sound like a fool repeating everything she says, but I'm really not grasping what she's trying to tell me. Georgia can't get any more words out from the sound of it, she's sobbing so hard. There's a scuffle at the other end and then a new voice comes on.

It's a doctor who explains that Max had been brought into the emergency room after taking an overdose and that they're very sorry but it was too late. They tried everything they could but were unable to save him. I listen to the words, but they sound like something you'd see on a tired hospital drama, not something to expect to hear about a guy I last saw a few hours ago. Max wouldn't do this; he's stronger than this. I try to tell the doctor that they must have the wrong man, but he assures me that there's no mistake. He tells me that Georgia is in a bad way and as she has no relatives close by he asks if there is any chance that I could come and pick her up. I agree.

I'm on autopilot all the way to the hospital. I manage to ring Cameron on route and let him know what's happened. He offers to call the rest of the guys for me and meet me at Max's house.

I pull up into the parking lot of the hospital and sit there for ten minutes trying to get my head around it all. Trying to put on a brave face for Georgia. I've failed. I've let my team down. I let Max down.

CHAPTER TEN

DECLAN - PRESENT TIME

I'm sitting in an anonymous hotel room and I've no idea how I got here, or even where here is. I've woken from yet another nightmare, and I can't tell which parts of it are real, and which parts of it are not. The half empty bottle of Jack Daniels on the nightstand clues me into the fact I had to drink myself to sleep yet again.

The clock throws out a faint glow as it clicks over to three am. Why does that time seem important? Snatches of conversations, glimpses of memory start to return and as the events of last night become clear again I'm ashamed of myself.

What the fuck have I become? A few months ago I was a Sergeant commanding a group of guys I loved like brothers. I was good at my job. Then one morning it all went to shit. That one morning destroyed lives, and I was powerless to stop it. I wish I hadn't killed that young boy now, I should have let him kill me, but would that have saved Max?

I can't seem to find reason or logic in anything. I can't even think of a reason why I should wake up, why I should be alive. Maybe Max was right, he thought we'd all be better off without him, and right now, I think everyone would be better off without me.

That's the Jack Daniels talking; at least I hope it is. I try and do a mental calculation of the pros and cons of staying alive. The only thing that is keeping me alive right now is that I haven't got a gun to shoot myself with.

There's a click as the clock turns to 3.02am. I can't think about this now, I'm so exhausted, I need to sleep. Picking up the bottle of Jack Daniels I drink myself back into oblivion. I'll think about this later.

CHAPTER ELEVEN

DECLAN

The hot shower washes away the sweat from my troubled nights sleep, but it does nothing to cleanse me of the self-loathing I'm feeling right now. I've downed the contents of a full bottle of Jack Daniels and the only side effect is a fuzzy mouth. I've got to stop drinking like this. It's a downward spiral. Gran would be furious if she could see me now. I promised her I'd pull my act together and I'm already failing her.

There's a knock at the door as I step out of the bathroom wrapped in the too small towel. It's Cameron, and like the friend he is he's bearing gifts, hot black coffee and bacon sandwiches. I mentally toss up the pros and cons of letting him in, knowing I'll get a tongue-lashing and unwelcome home truths but the rumbling from my stomach wins out.

"What happened?" he looks me up and down appraisingly. He shrugs his shoulders so I'm guessing he's not impressed with what he sees. I didn't look in the mirror this morning but I can imagine what he sees. Dark shadows under my eyes, unshaven stubble and no light behind my eyes at all, just dark pools of self-pity.

"I fucked up, Cam." I sag onto the mattress of the bed. I hadn't realised I was hungry till he passed me the bacon sarnie and I devoured it in a few bites. The hot coffee sates my thirst a little.

"Where the fuck have you been man? I've been calling you for three days." I look up at Cam in surprise. Three days? It can't be.

"What day is it?" I ask.

"It's Friday. Where the fuck have you been and why are you holed up in this shithole?" He looks confused. Shit. I'm confused. I've lost two days. Max's funeral was on Tuesday, surely today should be Wednesday?

"Friday?" I question. "You're having me on right? Today's Wednesday."

"Declan, what happened to you man? No one's seen you since the funeral on Tuesday. Georgia said you had some sort of nightmare and shot off and no one's heard from you since." His phone sounds a text message and he looks at the screen. "Oh yeah, you'd better give your Gran a call, she's having a shit fit to put it mildly."

I groan. I've just about convinced my Gran I'm pulling myself together and now I've lost two days in a drunken stupor again. She's going to ream my ass that's for sure. Cam is probably my closest friend, but how much can I tell him without making myself sound like I'm going insane?

"I fucked up, Cam." I whisper. "I don't know what happened, but I fucked up man." Involuntarily my body starts to shake, it's like a shiver runs through me and I can't control it. It's so bad I almost spill the hot coffee, but Cam reaches over and takes it from me, placing it on the nightstand.

Cam moves closer to me on the bed and puts his arm around me in a comforting gesture, it's my undoing, and big hard man that I am, I break down and cry on my friend's shoulder. Cam says nothing; he just sits there rubbing his hand on my back until I'm done. He lets me release it all without judging me.

"You need to get help, Declan. You can't bottle all this shit up and not expect to blow." He tells me. "We went through some bad shit, but you saved us, its done now. We're home, and we're safe." He talks quietly, soothingly, as though he was talking to a troubled child.

"I didn't save Max." I tell him. "I let him down, I should have been there for him." Guilt is eating me up, so is fear. "Every time I close my eyes I'm back there, in that Nary. I see that boys face." The shakes are back again, but Cam doesn't let go. He just sits there and talks to me quietly and calmly.

I honestly don't remember what he says to me, just the soothing tone. Eventually the shakes ease off.

"I'm not going to lose you, Declan." He states. "We're not going to lose you. We lost Max, and we're not losing anyone else." Cam reaches over and lifts my head so that I'm looking him in the eyes. "You're our leader, Declan. You're one strong motherfucker when you want to be, I need you to remember that. Now what's this all about?"

Slowly I talk Cameron through the nightmares, the panic attacks, even sleeping with Georgia and almost strangling her. The whole time he just sits there, I can't read him, but I don't think I see any judgement in his eyes either.

"You might want to ring Georgia and say sorry. That was a pretty shitty thing to do running out on her." I laugh; I can't help it. Out of everything I just told him that's the bit he picks up on.

"I think running out on her was the least of it." I mutter. He's right though, I do need to ring her and apologise.

"You need to ring your Gran first though, she's been blowing up my phone with messages." He grimaces as yet another text message tone sounds. He looks me up and down again. "Go grab another shower and a shave, make yourself look human and I'll go get more coffee and bacon. I'll let your Gran know I've found you, and once you're cleaned up you can ring her and let her know you're okay." He pats me on the back as he rises from the bed and starts typing on his phone.

"You'd better be here when I get back." He warns me as he walks out of the door.

CHAPTER TWELVE

DECLAN

I'm starting to feel more human thanks to Cam bringing coffee and food. I've shaved and washed my hair, now the guy looking back at me in the mirror looks a little more like me, although he still looks rough.

"So what are you going to do?" Cam asks me. "You need to get help."

I balk at the idea of sitting in a room with some head shrink. It's not me. There's got to be some other way of getting back to me.

"I don't know, Cam." I answer honestly. "I think I just need to get away for a while. Maybe go on a road trip with the bike."

I've always loved being out on the bike, hopefully that will help me get my head back in the right place.

"And what if that doesn't work?" Cam has a knack of asking the questions you don't want to answer. As much as I love him as a friend, right now I'm not his biggest fan.

"I don't know." I admit. Cam seems to consider this; he gives it a few minutes before he replies.

"I'll go with you. I've got a friend out near Mildura I was going to go see, old army buddy of my Dad's. Instead of flying I guess I could go on a road trip with you. It'll be a nice trip along the coastal highway, probably take us the best part of a week though." I can see him mentally calculating the route.

"Where's Mildura?" I ask. I've never heard of it.

"Well, we're actually going to Severed, it's outside of Mildura in Victoria." He smiles.

"We haven't been on the bikes in how long?" I ask. "And you want to ride to the other side of the country?" I laugh at the absurdity of it.

"Come on, Declan. You know you want to." Cam smirks. He's right. I do want to. A week on the bike, along the coastal highway stopping off in little towns along the way sounds like just what I need right now.

CHAPTER THIRTEEN

DECLAN

Gran really chewed me out on the phone, and I deserved it. I'd promised her that I'd got my act together then fallen big time. It was only after she spoke to Cam and he assured her he'd take care of me for her that she calmed down, relenting on her threats of having me committed for my own good. She's always had a soft spot for Cam. I'm grateful to my friend, as I'm damned sure my Gran would have followed through on her threat to have me admitted to hospital.

The route that Cam is thinking of is just over 3,000 kilometres. We could do it in a couple of days I guess if we rode hard, but we've decided to take it more slowly and appreciate it, probably taking the best part of a week to get to Severed instead. Being the awkward bugger that I am I suggest starting off further down the coast and that adds in another 1,000 kilometres. The bike needs it I tell myself. It's more that I've missed the sea breezes and want to stay as close to the coast as I can for the journey.

The first day we're heading down to Albany via Bridgetown and Manijmup. I might be pushing it with five hours on the bike after so much time away, but I reckon the route will more than make up for it. Of course, Cam will do his best to outdo me. We may be great friends, but we're always competing against each other, one more push up, one more weight, one more kilometre before we quit.

We stop a couple of times en route for fuel be it for the bikes or our bodies, but early evening sees us cruising down the Princess Royal Harbour to our backpacker hotel for the night. The accommodation may be basic, but compared to the camp in Afghanistan it's downright luxurious. We're the oldest people in the place as it's full of students.

As night falls we're out on the deck listening to them jamming on guitars and a keyboard and enjoying a cold beer. My entire body aches from the ride, but it's a good ache. It's been great to be back out on the bike today. From where we're sitting we can see the view across the harbour. The aqua marine ocean contrasting against the vivid colours of the flowers planted around the garden. For the first time since I came home from Afghanistan I feel peace. Cameron has his eye on a pretty young thing and it's not long before the two of them have disappeared off to our room. Her friend keeps giving me her come on eyes, but I'm not interested. After what happened with Georgia I'm not sure I feel safe sleeping with anyone, and truth be told I'm not in the mood. I fall asleep in the chair listening to the strumming of some love song on the guitar, I think it might be Adele 'Someone like you', and for the first time in a long time, I sleep without nightmares.

CHAPTER FOURTEEN

DECLAN

Cam found me asleep on the chair in the early hours of the morning once his conquest had returned to her room. Rather than wake me he took the seat next to me and nodded off himself. We woke to the aroma of freshly made pancakes. Sleeping in the chair hasn't made the aches any better, and I've got a crick in my neck, but I feel rested. I can't remember the last time I woke feeling rested. Cam just gives me a nod as he eases his own aching body from his chair.

We're riding to Gibson today, another five hour ride, but a little more inland. The arid earth is contrasted by the bright blue sky dotted with cotton wool clouds and the dark green of the few trees offering meagre shade at the side of the highway. Just before we enter Gibson we stop off at Observatory Point, the lush green bushes cling to the cliffside and draw your eyes down to the bay of teal blue water and the rocks below. It's stunning views like this that are calming my troubled soul. We sit there a good half hour just enjoying the view before heading into Gibson where we're spending the night at the Gibson Soak Hotel. It's an historical country pub with cheap and cheerful accommodation and good food. Out back there's a garden full of Morton Bay fig trees offering welcome shade from the heat of the day where we enjoy yet another cold beer.

There's a much quieter vibe about this pub than the student accommodation last night, and that's fine with me. I'm enjoying the peace and tranquillity for a change. Perhaps that's what my body and mind craved, silence after the noise and madness of the past few months.

The third day sees us heading for Caiguna, much to Cam's disgust, as the town isn't licensed yet. The Roadhouse doesn't have any of the atmosphere of the previous two places, it's a 24 hour food and fuel stop for buses and coaches and has a more family feel. The noise from the children's playground grates on my nerves and I have a bad night's sleep here. This was a mistake.

The next day we agree we'll push ourselves for eight hours to reach Ceduna and cross into Southern Australia. Last night did neither of us any favours. The good thing about todays route is that we're back on the coastal road, so whilst we're travelling further and longer, we've got an amazing view for most of the journey.

The East West motel in Ceduna has a swimming pool. The relief in my muscles when I enter the cool water is heaven after such a long day on the bike. We take the short walk down to the beach where we find a bar to spend the night and enjoy a good steak.

As usual Cameron picks up one of the tourists, this time heading off to her hotel, as it's a little fancier than ours. They leave me to entertain her friend. I'm tired and achy despite my swim and not really in the mood for company, but a few beers and half a bottle of Jack Daniels finds us back at my hotel.

Clarice or Claire, I can't remember her name right now, turns her nose up at the basic room. I can tell from the clothes she's wearing that someone has money, probably Daddy I'm guessing. I reckon she's slumming it with me to get one over on him for curbing her spending after her last credit card bill. I seem to recall something being said about this trip being a poor substitute for shopping in New York.

Right now, I don't care. Whatever her name is she's got my cock hard, rubbing her long nails against me through the denim of my jeans. With one hand she makes easy work of my belt and the buttons of my jeans and reaches in to wrap her fingers around my hard length. She slithers down my body to her knees, pulling my cock from my boxers and pushing my jeans around my ankles. Her hot mouth takes me in and I groan with pleasure. I may not be able to recall her name, but whoever she is certainly knows how to give a blowjob. Her tongue laps at the end of my cock before trailing up and down my length. There's a hint of teeth grazing my cock as she draws me in deeper, and her hand is pumping away at the part of me that doesn't fit into her tiny mouth.

I know I'm tired, but suddenly the sight of her on her knees in front of me just feels cheap and tacky. There's nothing erotic about this whole scene, from the cheap motel room to the fake tits that are bouncing around under her skimpy top and the dark roots in her overly blonde hair. I pull away suddenly.

"What the fuck?" She complains, rising to her feet.

"I'm sorry. I just can't." I turn my back on her and sink onto the bed.

"Fucking wimp." She screeches as she grabs her bag and slams out of the room. I sink back onto the bed, relief washing over me. I feel like I had a narrow escape, but why the fuck did I turn her down? What's wrong with me?

CHAPTER FIFTEEN

DECLAN

I've kind of lost track of the days here; I try and mentally count on my fingers and think we're on day five of our journey. I had a troubled night's sleep again after rejecting the blonde whose name I can't remember. Cameron crawled back in the early hours of the morning with a smug grin on his face and smelling of cheap perfume. Good for him. What's wrong with me that I don't want that anymore?

We look at the map and contemplate doing the final run through to Severed today, but it's a ten-hour slog and we're both starting to feel the wear of long days on the road so agree to stop off in Port Pirie overnight. Cam had been open about when we'd arrive in Severed and that was fine with his friend.

I missed moving away from the coastal road, but at least Port Pirie was on the river. It's a very industrial town though thankfully the motor inn we've booked for the night is quiet despite being on the highway. It's a comfortable bed and I fall asleep quickly, although I'm dragged awake by Cam after suffering yet another nightmare.

The journey has helped, most nights I'm exhausted and sleep right through, but a few nights he's had to wake me from nightmares. Luckily I haven't tried to hurt him when he's woken me; I'm still haunted by almost strangling Georgia that night.

With the end of our journey in sight we don't waste time, grabbing a quick breakfast and coffee and stuffing the panniers with sandwiches for lunch before heading off for our final journey into Severed.

CHAPTER SIXTEEN

DECLAN

For someone who wanted to stay on the coast there's something about Severed that I find soothing. It's a small town with a simple high street that has a coffee shop, a general store and even a tattoo shop. Cam's friend runs the local bar and that's where we're going to be staying.

The edges of the wide streets are shaded and cool from the old buildings on either side, and every so often there's a large tree offering more shade. The people seem friendly enough from what I can see. There's nothing here that reminds me of Afghanistan and that's good.

It looks even smaller than Harvey; perhaps that's why I feel comfortable here. The bar has seen better days, but the beer is cold and the conversation is plentiful. Jim welcomes Cam warmly, wrapping him in a bear hug.

"I've known Cam since he was a wee baby sucking on his mothers tit." Jim chuckles. Cam goes three shades of red at that, making me laugh out loud at his discomfort. I think I'm going to get on well with Jim.

The place has a worn dance floor, a dining area and booths along one wall. The wooden bar has seen better days, the varnish long since worn away showing ring marks from bottles and glasses. I imagine this was a classy joint when it first opened, but that looks to have been quite a few years ago now.

Jim tells us that it's pretty quiet most of the time, although they've had a few incidents over the past year between a couple of local MC clubs. "Don't get me wrong, the Severed guys are a good bunch, real family values, but there was a bad apple over at Carnal who gave them a hard time." He sighs, remembering. "We lost a few good people this past year. Damn shame." He looks thoughtful for a moment before continuing. "But it's over and done with now, we're looking forward to getting back to normal."

"Normal sounds good to me, I'm not sure if I can remember what it feels like though." I laugh. Jim gives me a long look.

"You don't have to tell me, son. I've been there myself." I know very little about Jim, other than he served in the military with Cam's Dad. I can see that despite his friendly demeanour something still haunts him. Will that be me in thirty years? I hope not.

Jim shows us up to our rooms. It's basic, but spotlessly clean, although the shower could do with a little more oomph to it. Still, the slow trickle of warm water helps me rid the road dust from my weary body. I lie down on the bed while Cam has his shower and find myself being gently shaken awake by him. The rooms dark now, I must have fallen asleep.

"I didn't want to let you sleep any later mate, thought you could do with something to eat." Cam offers. I sit up groggily and reach for my watch. I've been asleep for several hours. I'm still tired, but not as tired as I was, and I realise it was dreamless sleep as well.

"What's on offer?" I question Cam.

"Steak, burger, barbecue?" He offers me a meat lover's selection.

"Good job I'm not a vegetarian." I laugh. "I'll take a steak I reckon."

The dining area is quiet, it's midweek and only a few drinkers are in the bar, pretty much keeping to themselves. The food is excellent, much better than I'd have expected for a small town like this. Jim leaves us to our meal while he serves at the bar.

"What's the story?" I ask Cam. He sees me watching Jim. "He's an old buddy of my Dad's and I think he needs help, but doesn't want to ask for it." He tells me. "He called me the other week and asked if I'd like to come for a visit and a catch up. I've not been out here for years, but there was something in his voice. I can't put my finger on it, but I felt like I needed to come see him, make sure he was okay." Cam watches the old man with affection. There's obviously some good history between them.

"He did say the town had been through a rough patch lately, do you think that's it?" I look down at my plate to find it's empty. I've devoured the whole thing. Looks like I got my appetite back as well.

"I don't know. I don't think it's that. I reckon if we stay around for a few days he'll let me know what's wrong. We can see if there's anything we can do to help him." Cam always seems to be the one who fixes things for people. He's probably the most sensitive of us all, often making things right before the rest of us have even twigged that they were wrong.

We chat about the town over dessert, home made apple pie and ice cream, it's almost as good as my Gran's. I can see I'm going to have to keep an eye on my weight whilst I'm here. Talk turns to the tattoo shop and Cam asks if I'm planning on any more ink.

"Not yet, I'll get a piece to remember Max by, but not sure what I want yet." The thing with ink and me is that I'll spend forever deciding what I want, but once I have I get it done almost straight away. The design is important to me; I need to make sure it's just right. It means that I have less ink than the rest of the guys, especially Max, he was always the first to go get a new tattoo when we'd been out drinking heavily.

"You think about Max?" Cam asks quietly. "I still don't get why he did it." There's hurt in Cam's voice. It's a hurt we all feel. To have been so close to someone like we were with Max, for him then to turn us all away when we wanted to help. We're all struggling to come to terms with it.

"Yeah. I just wish there was something we could have done. If we'd pushed to go see him sooner..." My voice falls away. We can all wish as much as we like, but it isn't going to change anything. It won't bring Max back. It won't make us whole again.

Before we can get any more maudlin Jim comes over to clear the table. "You not got some pretty young thing to help you out Jim?" Cam teases. Jim's face falls. Cam obviously hit a nerve.

"I had." He pauses, wistfully. "Danni, lovely young girl. She got caught up in the trouble, must be three months now since we buried her and her man." Jim seems to give himself a shake. "Enough sad talk, what are you guys drinking? I want to catch up on all your shenanigans young Cam." He ends on a laugh.

I'm not sure we're ready to talk about our shenanigans either, but Jim joins us with a bottle of Jack Daniels and we spend the rest of the evening reminiscing over Cam's childhood escapades and misadventures on his trips to Severed.

CHAPTER SEVENTEEN

HOLLY

I'm happy sitting in the back corner of the bar, minding my own business and nursing a drink when I spot the hot guy. Or should I say, hot guys. There are two of them, although it's the sandy haired one who has my interest. His dark haired friend looks good enough, but there's something about his blue eyed companion.

Jim obviously knows the dark haired guy, although he doesn't look familiar to me. I think I'd have noticed him before now. I've sneaked out of the clubhouse and away from my overly protective uncle and his friends. They seem to want to treat me with kid gloves all the time, but they've got to let me get on with my life at some point.

It's three months since we buried my brother and my best friend. I still can't believe that I won't see either of them again. It's so unfair, after all that time we didn't talk to each other for us to make up and then lose them so quickly. I'm still struggling with the why. Some stupid crack whore who was hell bent on revenge and my crazy ex who took advantage of her messed up plan. Am I to blame? If I'd never met that loser would Justice still be dead? Would I have taken so long to make up with my best friend when I found out she was sleeping with my brother.

That was just the most recent trouble the club had suffered, turns out there'd been death threats and kidnap attempts before that. That's why I'm normally watched like a hawk. It's to keep me safe, but it feels more like a prison and a punishment than anything else. It's why I'm sitting here in the shadows, out of sight. That's where I've been for the last few months, scared that if I let myself get close to anyone they'll be taken from me as well.

I swirl the straw around in my soft drink and go back to watching the strangers across the room.

CHAPTER EIGHTEEN

DECLAN

We've been in Severed for a couple of days just kicking back and enjoying the quiet pace when we finally get to the bottom of Jim's concerns. His sister lives in Derby, clear the other side of the country and she's got cancer. She lost her husband a few years ago and she's been diagnosed as terminal. Jim wants to spend what time she has left with her.

"As you can see, it's not exactly prime real estate." He sighs as he indicates the tired interior.

"You sure you want to sell?" Cam asks. "I could probably hang around for a few months and run the place for you." He offers.

"I need the money to help with her medical bills." Jim tells us. "I don't have anything left in the bank." He looks beaten.

"Have you had the place valued yet?" Cam asks at the same time as me. It would be funny if Jim didn't look so beaten down.

Jim mentions a figure that seems pretty cheap to me, granted the place needs an overhaul, but it still seems good value for money compared to what he could have asked in Perth, or even Harvey.

"Have you listed it with the agent yet?" I don't recall seeing a for sale board outside.

"No, not yet, I've been trying to work out whether to sink some money into it and then sell it, or just sell it as is. I guess I just want to get over to Derby sooner rather than later." He takes a long slow drink before placing his glass neatly back on the coaster on the table.

I spend the rest of the morning mulling things over and checking various things on my tablet. I've got an idea I want to run past Cam, see if he thinks it makes sense or not.

"Cam, you got a minute?" I call him over to the table I've been sitting at for most of the afternoon.

"Yeah, sure what's up mate?" He asks as he sits down next to me.

"I've been thinking about Jim's problem and I might have a solution." Cam looks at me with interest now.

"Yeah?"

"I'm thinking I might buy the place." I stop waiting to see Cam's reaction. He looks a little surprised, but I guess I did kind of come out of nowhere with this idea.

"You sure? I don't see you as a pub landlord somehow, especially with our background."

"It's because of our background." I can't help playing with the beer mat in my hands. It's getting a little tattered around the edges. "Everyone expects us to go into security work when we leave the Army, and I don't want that. I just want to slow down the pace a little, and I like it here. I've got enough money in the bank to buy this place and fix it up."

Cam looks at me, really looks at me as if he can see deep inside me. I know he's worried about me, and with my recent drinking history buying a pub might not be the best idea I've ever had, but somehow this feels right. He picks up his glass and raises it towards me. "In that case, go for it. I think you're right. It could be a good move for you." We clink glasses in a toast. "Do you need a partner?"

"It's your friend so I guess I can't say no, but I'm happy to do this on my own. I wasn't asking for a partner." Cam looks slightly relieved when I say this, I know this isn't the life he was looking for, but I also know he'd have done this with me if I asked him to.

"Well in that case I think we should go find Jim and tell him the good news." Cam laughs.

I look at the tablet in front of me, and just for a moment wonder if I'm doing the right thing. Then I look around the empty bar. I feel at home here, this is the right thing for me; it's the right place. It's a new future.

CHAPTER NINETEEN

DECLAN

My head is spinning at the speed at which things are happening. Jim practically snapped my hand off when I made him my offer. Luckily most of the legal stuff can be done online such as the title search, filing for the zoning certificate and filing for a drainage diagram. I've signed and completed so many forms I've lost track. There's stamp duty to pay, legal titles to transfer and of course conveyancers and solicitors who want a cut of the pie as well.

It was surprisingly easy, and perhaps should have taken longer for me to spend that obscene amount of money. That's technology for you. It's going to take a couple of weeks for it all to confirm, but the paperwork's completed and Jim's booked his flight. In just a few days this place will be legally mine.

Cam called Luke and he's given us the name of some reliable contractors who are able to come in at short notice and start gutting the place. Jim told us to go ahead, we don't have to wait for the paperwork. If it had been any one else I'd have exercised caution and waited for the signed and sealed contract, but it's Cam's friend and I'm on a reckless spree.

The hardest part was ringing Gran to tell her what I'm doing. I'd expected a lecture from her, especially at the rate we were moving along with the whole thing, but she surprised me.

"Declan, I'm going to miss you, why you had to decide to move to the opposite side of the country I don't know, but if this feels right for you, then you have my support." It's only when I hear her say this that I realise how far away I'm going to be from her. At least when I was in Afghanistan I knew I was coming back to be with her, now I'm moving across country.

"You'll have to come see the place when I've done it up, Gran." I invite her. We both know she's too old and stubborn to leave her farm, so I'll have to make sure I make regular trips back home.

"Yeah, yeah. You're the young one here, you can come see me." She laughs. "Besides, your boys are all here so you can visit us all at the same time." My Gran always has a logical reason, and she always seems to win any discussion with her logic. I'm going to miss her.

"Cam's staying on an extra couple of weeks to give me a hand, and I think Luke might come and give me his advice on the refit." It's only been just over a week, but I miss the guys already.

"Good, good. Get Luke to come see me before he comes and I'll send you some proper food." She laughs. Gran doesn't think anywhere serves proper food outside of her kitchen.

"Well, now you mention it I don't suppose you fancy sharing some of your recipes with me do you?" I ask, already knowing the answer.

"Pffft and piddle young man as you well know. You'll get my recipes when I'm dead and gone, until then you just have to come visit if you're missing my cooking." She laughs.

"It was worth a try."

Cam walks into the room, indicating that there's a call for me on his phone. I say my goodbyes to my Gran and take the phone from him.

"Hey, Declan. I've booked a flight for the morning, bringing you some brochures and stuff on the type of fittings I think you'll need and I'll help you interview the contractors." Luke offers.

"Thanks for this, I know you're busy with your own projects." I'm grateful to have his input on the project, if nothing else I know he'll save me money, as he won't let me employ the wrong guys or purchase the wrong fixtures and fittings.

"It's no problem. I've been worried about you, we all have. Besides, I can't wait to see this project of yours that's got you moving so far away from us." He laughs.

Everyone keeps reminding me how far away I'm moving from what I've known, perhaps it's because of the lack of permanent residence in the Army, but I don't see it as a problem, more as a challenge to embrace. It's not like there isn't an airport close by after all. I can go home and visit when I want. I'm still in the same country at least.

I end the call with Luke and go back to flicking through the websites on bar interiors. I don't want to employ a designer, it's only a small pub and I'm pretty sure between Luke and I that we can come up with something suitable for the locals and my own tastes.

CHAPTER TWENTY

DECLAN

Luke's visit was short and sharp, but we got a lot accomplished. The crew we hired have almost finished, the place is certainly transformed. I've kept as much of the character as I could, and added in a few modern touches to make life easier like a dishwasher for the glasses behind the bar and a new kitchen that's more suitable for catering than the small set up that Jim had.

I've retained a couple of the staff that Jim had, but he told me he still hadn't replaced the barmaid who'd been killed and he thinks that I'll need more bodies, if only to handle the curiosity of the locals who'll come visit once I re-open.

I almost don't hear the banging on the door over the noise of the drill and the hammering. When I open the door I'm surprised to see a petite girl wearing a white vest, denim skirt and a look of shock on her face.

"Can I help you?" I ask her as I check her out.

"Erm." She stutters, "Hi, I'm here for the job?"

"Oh." I look her over again. She doesn't look like a barmaid. "Have you done any bar work before?"

"A little." She replies. "More waitressing though." She goes on to say something about helping her parents out at parties. I don't believe she's got any experience, but she looks so nervous and desperate that I decide to give her a chance.

"I'm Declan, the new owner of this place." I invite her in.

We make small talk on the way in, and I tell Lucy that I was looking for a career change when I bought the bar. That was obviously a mistake as she innocently asks what I used to do. Shit. I don't want to talk about my past. I'm a little curt in my reply to her.

"I came here to start a new future, not discuss my past." I snap.

"A new future sounds pretty good to me right now as well." She replies. I soften a little at her response. Sounds like Lucy has some problems, and the protective side of me comes out.

Lucy jumps at a loud bang the contractors make, she looks nervous until I explain about the refurbishment. I offer to show her around whilst I interview her. I'm not exactly used to interviewing bar staff so I ask the basics. All the time she's showing interest in the work going on around us, and answers my questions smoothly and comfortably until I ask her about her last position. I can see her whole body tense as she tells me she was fired.

I can't imagine what a little thing like her could have done to merit being fired and laughingly tell her so. That's when she lets me see her inner firecracker.

"Little?" She snaps. She's easily five seven so I guess she isn't really little, but compared to the guys I'm used to hanging around with she seems petite.

I apologise to her, but my mood soon darkens when she explains she was fired for slapping her over friendly boss. I hate guys who take advantage of their position. I re-assure her that she'll have nothing like that to worry about from me. She seems a little more comfortable now that conversation is out of the way and I continue to show her around. She seems overly excited about the new dance floor that I'm installing.

By the time we're back in the main bar I've decided to take a chance on Lucy. I'm pretty sure she doesn't have the experience I need, but she's got a nice personality and I think she'd get on well with the locals.

"Really?" Her face lights up in delight when I give her the good news. She blushes when I tell her that it will be good to have a pretty face around here.

I ask her to come in Wednesday morning so she can help set up and get some training in before we re-open on Friday and she leaves with a huge grin on her face. It sounds silly, but our little encounter has put a huge smile on my face as well.

CHAPTER TWENTY ONE

DECLAN

Tonight's the grand re-opening and the place is packed, although the half price drinks offer might have something to do with it. I look around the busy bar and feel a huge sense of achievement. I'm just sorry that my guys couldn't make it for the opening; even Cam had to go home, although they've all promised that they'll be out to visit soon.

I've given my new barmaid the night off, I think she needs more experience before she tackles a crowd of this size considering the number of glasses she broke on her first day. I'll keep her on the quieter day shifts for now until she gets up to speed. She's coming in tonight with a bunch of her friends, I'm looking forward to meeting them.

I've walked the room a few times when I notice Lucy and her friends at a table. They're pretty hard to miss; aside from the fact that some of them are absolutely stunning they're easily one of the loudest groups in here this evening.

"How's my favourite bar maid doing?" I greet Lucy with a kiss on her cheek.

She goes around the table introducing me to her friends. I forget their names apart from the girl she calls Holly. She's breath taking. I find myself looking at her for a moment too long and don't miss the blush as she notices. I try and cover it by calling over one of the bar staff to take a drinks order and offer the girls drinks on the house for the rest of the night. It could be an expensive gesture, but I think it will be worth it.

I watch the girls discreetly for the rest of the evening, trying to figure out the dynamics and see if Holly is with anyone. It's obvious that some of them are with the table of bikers on the other side of the room, especially when the DJ plays the last track and a few of them pair off for a slow dance.

I don't miss Lucy's wistful look at the biker who hasn't left the table. She leaves the dance floor to go sit with a couple of the other girls, including Holly. I'm tempted to ask Holly to dance, but I don't fancy my chances if she's with one of those bikers.

Lucy and her group leave on shaky heels and with a very noisy goodbye. I dread to think of the hangovers they're going to be facing in the morning. They're the last to leave and I lock the door behind them with a sense of satisfaction. The night's gone well.

CHAPTER TWENTY TWO

HOLLY

The mood in the clubhouse was sombre this morning, mainly due to the amount of alcohol consumed last night. Most of them were still in bed when I sneaked out. I need some fresh air. I'm tired of feeling trapped and cooped up.

The main street is quiet this early on a morning, and I breathe in the cool fresh air with relief. There's no one watching over me. I call into the general store and pick up a magazine I probably won't read, I'll just flick through the pages, but it gives me something to do.

I'm shouting goodbye over my shoulder instead of looking where I'm going as I head out of the general store and find myself smacking into a brick wall. Well it feels like a brick wall.

It's a guy. I look up into those brilliant blue eyes and see that it's Declan, the new owner from the bar.

"I'm so sorry." I splutter, my hands on his chest for a moment too long. I see the smirk on his face as he spots them and pull them back quickly.

"That's okay, Holly isn't it?" He has a warm smile that lights up his face. I've heard the guys back at the clubhouse muttering about Declan. No one seems to know who he is or where he's come from and that bothers them. He seems harmless enough to me.

"I was just popping in for a tin of coffee." He tells me, and then seems to change his mind. "Don't suppose you fancy joining me at the coffee shop for a decent latte do you? I hate drinking on my own." His smile is so earnest and safe that I can't help but accept.

"Sounds like a great idea."

Declan walks by my side as we cross the street to the coffee shop, putting his hand on my arm to guide me through the door when he opens it for me. He pulls the chair out for me at a table in the back of the shop and then goes to the counter to order for us both, after asking me what I want. He's a gentleman as well I note to myself, I'm pretty sure the Neanderthals back at the club wouldn't have treated me this nicely. It's not that they're not good guys, they just seem to always take control of any situation involving me. I hate losing my identity like that.

When Declan returns he's carrying a tray with our drinks and a couple of blueberry muffins as well.

"Hope you don't mind sharing a muffin with me as well." He smiles, offering one to me. "I missed breakfast and I hate eating alone."

"They're my favourite!" I grin.

We spend an hour in the coffee shop talking about everything and nothing. I get the impression he doesn't want to talk about his past, and neither do I so we stay on safe subjects like music and movies that we love. I like this guy. We seem to have a lot of tastes in common, and he's hot. What's not to like?

Declan's phone rings and he looks at the number curiously, obviously not recognising it.

"Hi, this is Declan." He greets the caller in a formal tone. Ooh I like that voice, it sends shivers through me.

"Cowboy?" He questions. I look up then, wondering what Cowboy could be ringing Declan for. He laughs then at whatever's said. "No problem, I'll switch her shift with one of the guys and give her a call and let her know." He's still laughing when he hangs up.

"That was Cowboy. Odd choice of name, but he rang to say your friend Lucy isn't feeling so hot this morning and won't be able to maker her shift." He gives me a warm smile. "I'm afraid I need to get back to the bar and sort it out." He looks apologetic. "I enjoyed this," he gestures to our now empty coffee cups. "Do you think we could do it again sometime?"

"I'd like that." I answer coyly. I would like that, a lot, but I'm careful of showing too much interest in this guy. I've not got the best track record and I'm pretty sure the guys back at the clubhouse wont approve.

Declan swaps numbers with me before walking me back to my truck. He gives me a peck on the forehead as he says goodbye. Is it wrong that I wish it had been a kiss on the lips?

I turn the key in the ignition and set off back to the clubhouse. My plans for the magazine are now defunct. I'm going to go back, lie on my bed and think dirty thoughts about this new stranger instead.

CHAPTER TWENTY THREE

DECLAN

The Sunday lunch crowd is keeping us busy today. Lucy seems to be over her hangover, but there's something not quite right with her and I can't figure it out until a couple of bikers walk in and Lucy glares at one of them before turning away. Man trouble. It's not my place to interfere, but I'll have a chat with her at the end of her shift and make sure she's okay.

"Gentlemen, how can I help you? Table for two?" I walk over and greet them. One of the guys gives me the once over and doesn't look pleased with what he sees. That's fine by me; I've come up against worse. He's the guy that Lucy was ignoring.

"Do you have a moment?" The other guy asks. "We'd like a little chat if you can spare the time?"

I catch the non-speaker watching Lucy closely. I can see he has feelings for her.

"She's a good worker." I inform him. "I'd hate to see her get hurt." He doesn't like that and his colleague has to hold him back slightly.

"I'd never hurt her." He growls at me.

"She's family." His friend tells me. "We take care of ours." I can hear the unspoken threat.

I nod in understanding and lead the guys back to my office. I get the impression this isn't a conversation about the merits of roast pork versus roast beef somehow.

I sit on the edge of my desk facing them and ask how I can help.

The guy who's done most of the talking introduces himself as Angel, Vice President of the local MC club. The other guy with him is Cowboy, the one who rang me to tell me Lucy was ill yesterday. Angel looks me straight in the eye when he tells me how they keep an eye on the town and the people here, and that recently a bad element has come into town.

I take a deep breath before I reply, getting a hold on my anger. "And you think I'm that bad element?"

"I didn't say that." Angel replies. He goes on to ask me what I'm doing in Severed. My answers are brief and clipped. It's none of their business, but I don't want to rub these guys up the wrong way.

I lose it when they tell me they don't' allow drugs in Severed.

"I don't allow drugs in my bar." Angel continues to probe, but I'm not answering his questions. I think it's pretty obvious I'm against drugs, but that's as much as I'm prepared to let on. I came her to escape my past, not be reminded of it.

I tell them about the dealer I found in the bar on opening night, and that he won't be returning any time soon. I don't tell them that I left him a bloodied mess out back, but I think they can tell that it wasn't just an idle threat in conversation that he left with.

The conversation gets a little easier from then, and I can see that the club are really concerned about drugs being dealt in Severed. I've got contacts that I can call on to help the situation and allude to that, without giving away who they are. I don't want them to know about my military history, or the contacts I still have outside of that.

I've just moved here. I can't watch anyone else I care about, or become close to kill themselves because of drugs. I won't.

By the time the guys leave my office we've reached an agreement. We're not going to be best buddies, but we understand and respect each other.

I let Cowboy know that I'll make sure Lucy gets home safely after her shift. "From the look she gave you when you walked in I'm guessing you're not in her good books at the moment." I laugh.

Lucy makes a point of waving at Angel as they leave, but turns her back on Cowboy. I'm going to have to find out what the poor guy did to deserve that treatment, but right now I've got some calls to make.

I need to find out what the hell is going on in Severed.

CHAPTER TWENTY FOUR

DECLAN

I hang up the phone and sigh. This is not good. I contacted an ex-army buddy Chris, who runs his own security firm out of Melbourne, to ask him about the drug problems we're having in Severed. From everything he's seen so far he seems to think that this is more than some random drug dealer we're dealing with, but a large organised gang.

He's asked me to give him a few more days to look into it. I don't want this shit on my doorstep. I don't need this shit.

What I do want is to see that gorgeous blonde Holly again. I pick up my phone and send her a text.

> *DECLAN: How do you fancy an evening picnic with me tonight?*

HOLLY: Sounds fun, meet you at yours at 8 with my truck?

DECLAN: I look forward to it :-)

I know I need to concentrate on the drug problem in Severed, but for one night I'm going to allow myself to lead a normal, civilian life. I need it.

I'm glad Holly's bringing her pick up, I don't think a picnic basket would fit on the bike. Who am I kidding? I've travelled half way around Australia on this bike; it's got more than enough storage. But, I can't lay a blanket out on the top of a bike in the same way I can in the back of a pick up truck. I foresee some stargazing laid out next to Holly this evening.

HOLLY

I put the phone back in my pocket, a silly grin on my face. Eve gives me a questioning look.

"Nothing, just going to see a friend later." I tell her. Eve's look turns into a knowing smirk. That girl is too switched on for her own good. When she sees the panic on my face she reassures me.

"Don't worry, Holly. I won't say anything to the guys. I've seen how they've been treating you like a fragile doll these past few months. I can't stand it when they do it to me." I reach over and hug Eve. She's a breath of fresh air in the club, and I love her and her friend Elle. They help keep me grounded and sane. They're strong characters; they've survived some pretty bad shit since they became involved in the club and they've not let it beat them. If anything it's made them stronger.

"Are you going to tell me who this friend is?" Eve enquires.

"Not yet," I hesitate. "It's early days. If it looks like it's going to turn into anything then I'll let you know." I promise.

"Okay, but make sure you've got your phone with you, and if you need anything promise me you'll ring me." She smiles.

"Absolutely."

"You'd best go check out that wardrobe of yours and let me know if you need to borrow any short skirts." Eve offers.

"It's okay," I smile. "I think I've got this one covered."

DECLAN

The chef has made us up a picnic that could probably feed the five thousand. Okay, I may be exaggerating, but there's plenty of food. I remembered to go over to the bakery and buy blueberry muffins for Holly, as I know she loves them.

I pack the last of the bottles of coke and beer in the cooler, and check my watch for the fifth time in as many minutes. It's almost eight. I'm grinning like a schoolboy, and it hasn't gone unnoticed by Lucy.

"What are you up to?" She teases me. I offer to tell her if she spills the beans on her and Cowboy and that soon shuts her up. There's definitely something between them judging from the blush she gets on her face whenever I mention his name. I'm just grateful she didn't call me on my bluff. I'm not ready to tell anyone about Holly yet.

I grab the cooler and head out of the back door of the kitchen to sit and wait on the stoop. I've barely sat down when Holly's truck pulls into the yard.

I motion for her to stay in the drivers seat as I load the cooler and blankets into the bed of the truck, before pulling myself up into the passenger seat. I almost draw in a breath as I see her long bare legs peeping out of the almost not there denim skirt. She's wearing a cotton check shirt that's tied around the waist and shows off her cleavage under the tight white vest top. Shit. I I've got a hard on already just from looking at her.

She smirks as she sees me trying to adjust my jeans, pulling out of the yard and asking me if I have a destination in mind.

"I've not been here long enough to know where's where." I confess. "You got any back roads next to an old creek or something?"

"How cliché." She giggles. "I know just the spot." She heads out of town and takes a side road. Pretty soon we're on a dirt track lined with trees. It's peaceful out here, no noise from passing vehicles, just the buzz of the odd insect and the quiet burble of the water in the creek as it flows around some small rocks.

Holly parks the truck, and before I can get round to open her door for her she's jumped down and standing at the side of the water.

"I love it here. My brother and I used to play here when we were little and visiting my Uncle." I can see she's lost in a good memory. I stand behind her and enclose her in my arms, not wanting to disturb the moment.

"I have a creek like that back on my Gran's farm." I tell her about playing there with my friends on hot summers days. They're good memories.

"Won't you miss your Gran, living this far away from her?"

"No, I'm used to not seeing much of her. I used to travel a lot. Besides, she's only a plane ride away. I'll probably see more of her than before." I know that I'll make the effort to see my Gran.

Holly sinks further back into my arms. This feels comfortable and right. "Why did you used to travel?" I knew she'd want to know more of my past, I'm just not sure if I want to tell her it, and if I do, how much I want to share.

"Work." I try and escape the conversation. "Tell me about you first?" I encourage her. "Then I'll share my deep, dark secrets with you." She begins to laugh, but something stops her. It's a memory. I can see the smile fall from her face. "Let's get this picnic set up, and you can tell me what you feel like sharing." I offer.

Holly looks a little more comfortable once we've got the picnic laid out on the blanket. Slowly, over the next couple of hours she tells me about her ex, about her brother Justice, and how she lost him and her friend recently. I can sense the guilt in her.

I don't tell Holly everything, but I do tell her that I used to be in the Army, and that I lost a friend as a result of an IED on our last patrol. I can't bring myself to tell her about killing the young boy, or sleeping with Georgia, or about Max taking his own life. It's not much, but it's the first time I've shared any of my feelings.

From the sound of it both of our nightmares share the same timescale. It's spooky. If I believed in fate I'd say we'd been thrown together to heal each other.

The food was finished and the rubbish packed away a while ago, meaning we're just laid on our backs, side by side on the blanket. The stars have come out now. The sky is perfectly clear, lit by a thousand white lights. Just laying here like this is calming. It's odd but I feel comfortable with Holly. We don't need conversation; both happy just to lay here in each other's company and contemplate the night sky.

HOLLY

Declan is still a mystery to me, but not as much as he was before this evening. I can sense that there's more to the story than he's told me, but like me, he finds it hard to share.

As hard as it is to talk about Danni and Justice, and everything that happened, I never felt that Declan held me responsible for any of it while we spoke. He just held my hand and nodded in understanding.

He's a sweet guy, although I'm guessing with his military background he'd hate me calling him that. He even remembered that I love blueberry muffins.

It's so peaceful here; I can feel the heat from his body lying beside me on the blanket. I think I could fall asleep here and not have nightmares.

Declan reaches over to brush the hair away from my face; his touch is gentle and tender as he pushes the stray lock behind my ear. His finger traces down the side of my cheek, down my neck and to the swell of my breasts where he pauses.

He moves his hand and lifts my chin towards his, planting a soft kiss on my lips. I kiss him back. The kiss deepens between us, soon we're biting lips and then his tongue invades my mouth. I can feel his kisses all the way through my body. I'm on fire. Between us my shirt has been removed, and I've almost wrestled his t-shirt over his head. Holy shit. This guy has abs.

He's a lot leaner and more toned than the guys back at the clubhouse, but his body vibrates strength and energy. I trace my nails down his chest towards that seductive V that disappears into his jeans. Meanwhile he's tracing his hands up inside my skirt.

We're making out like a couple of teenagers and I love it. His hand reaches the silk of my panties, teasing me. It would be rude not to reciprocate so I undo the belt and buttons of his jeans, pushing my hand inside his boxers. He's hard as steel already. His cock is pulsing beneath my fingers as I wrap my hand around him.

His fingers push my panties aside and he eases a finger into me. Fuck. That feels good. I'm already wet for him as he pushes his finger in deeper. His thumb meanwhile is working on my clit. I'm trying to move my hand up and down his cock, but the distraction from his fingers and thumb is too much. I just clench my fist tight around him as he takes me to the brink of my orgasm. Holy shit. The sky has nothing on the stars that explode behind my eyes as I peak.

I struggle to draw in a breath. That was amazing. Declan hasn't stopped though. He's pushed my skirt up around my waist and removed my underwear. All the while he's continued to kiss me.

He pulls back, an unspoken question in his eyes. "Yes." I whisper. "I need you." He moves away from me for a moment to remove his jeans and fish a condom from his wallet. I feel the chill as his body leaves mine. He's quickly back at my side, already sheathed. I gasp as he enters me for the first time. The feeling is indescribable; we fit together so perfectly. He eases further into me then starts thrusting. His cock feels like steel as he pushes deeper and deeper. I arch my back to meet his thrusts, wrapping my legs around his back.

He takes a hand and pulls my left leg down, straightening it out and pinning it under his. My right leg is still wrapped around him. In this position we're almost side-by-side facing each other. It seems even more intimate than when he was above me. This time when he thrusts its deeper still. The angle feels like he's going to split me in two, but it doesn't hurt. Instead it's blissful.

He kisses me deeply, our tongues tangling, before pulling his head back to move down and draw my nipple into his mouth. He bites down lightly and the pain is exquisite. I cry out and I can't believe it when I feel his cock harden even more at the sound. He bites down a little harder the next time and my orgasm rushes through me. I scream out as I come. Seconds later he comes as well. The look on his face and the roar he lets out, as as he fills me with his come, is my undoing. I lay back, sated and with the hugest smug grin on my face.

He laughs when he sees my expression. "Well don't you look like the cat that got the cream."?

"Yep." I smirk, seeing a similar smug grin on his face. "So do you. That was fucking awesome!" I grin.

"Why thank you." He collapses on his back at the side of me.

We lay there under the stars letting the night air cool our overheated skin. It's dawn before we pack up the blanket, collect up our rubbish and get back in the truck to head home. We've made love several times, each time better and more mind blowing than the time before.

I'm going to have trouble walking tomorrow and it's going to be worth every single ache and pain.

CHAPTER TWENTY FIVE

DECLAN

I can't help walking around with a smug grin on my face all morning. Holly and I have exchanged several texts but not set up another date yet. I definitely want to see this girl again. The sex was amazing, but it's more than that. There's some sort of connection between us, when we're together I feel whole.

Another text sounds and I smile at the message she's sent me.

HOLLY: My abs are killing me! I feel like we did a huge gym workout last night!

DECLAN: Well the gym is good for you; we'll have to arrange another session ;-)

HOLLY: Definitely! The sooner the better x

I'm about to think of some witty reply to send back when there's a commotion from the front of the bar. Something's happened outside judging by the fact most of my bar staff are rushing outside as well as some of the customers.

I head outside to see what's going on. The tattoo shop down the street looks to have a smashed front window. The bikes outside are on the ground.

"What the hell?" Josh, one of the barmen cries. "Not again!"

What does he mean not again? I pull Josh to one side and ask him. He tells me that three months ago, when the club had all the trouble, someone fell through the tattoo shop window and was killed. It was the woman who'd killed Danni.

The guys over at the Tattoo shop seem to have everything under control so I usher everyone back into the pub. I'll go over later and see what happened. For now I'm probably better off trying to minimise the whole thing in front of the staff and the customers. It's too much of a coincidence to me that they tell me we've got a drug problem in Severed and then their shop window and bikes get trashed.

I don't have to wait too long before a pissed off Angel comes into the bar with Cowboy and the tattooist Ink.

I usher them over to a quiet booth, away from eavesdroppers.

"So you had your window smashed and the tyres on all your bikes slashed?" I ask. "You boys sure lead interesting lives." I laugh.

Angel tells me that Ink and Cowboy had seen someone dealing drugs on the main street and confronted him. The guy had no shame and no intention of getting the hell out of Severed when they asked. I'm guessing they weren't very diplomatic in their asking. The dealer told them that his boss is in town now and they need to accept that. Shit. This isn't just some small town dealer working alone; it's an organised group of them at least.

I've left them to their drinking for a couple of hours when the pub doors fly open and one of their prospects comes rushing in to speak with Angel. Turns out it's the prospect they'd set to follow the dealer after their little encounter earlier. The poor kid lost him.

I exchange a look with Angel, the kid needs a break, he's obviously shit scared at sharing his failure with his boss. Angel nods; he's not a bad bloke after all. I pass the prospect a beer just as Angel's phone rings.

Angel answers then gulps down his drink, it looks like he's got to get out of here.

"We gotta run, Declan. Thanks for the beers."

I assure Angel it's no problem and promise to get in touch with my contacts again. We need to get to the bottom of this shit and fix it, sooner rather than later.

CHAPTER TWENTY SIX

DECLAN

I put the phone down in shock. I can't believe things have escalated so badly and so quickly.

That was Cowboy. There was an explosion at Carnal MC's clubhouse. The guys from Severed had gone there for a meeting to try and sort out this drug situation. The president of Carnal is dead, and the Severed MC president is in hospital in a critical condition.

The way Cowboy described the explosion, and the fact the perpetrator used grenades tells me we're dealing with a serious offender. They think the explosion was a result of the Carnal guys roughing up the dealer the Severed MC prospect lost the trail of yesterday.

This shit is serious. I'm just thankful none of the other Severed guys were seriously hurt. I've got to get in touch with Chris and see if he's found anything out that can help us. I'm going to be calling in a massive favour, but it can't be helped. I may have only just moved here, but I can't sit back and watch Severed be destroyed by drugs.

I think of Holly and how all this must be affecting her, then remember that her Uncle is Severed's president. Shit. She must be going through hell right now. I'm guessing she'll be at the hospital with her Aunt, but I need to talk to her, make sure she's okay.

The phone rings onto voicemail so I leave her a message letting her know it's me and the time. I'm not expecting to hear back from her any time soon, but the phone rings almost as soon as I put it down. It's her number.

"Hey." I ask gently. "How are you?" Such a stupid question at a time like this.

"I'm okay, still in shock." I can hear her sobbing quietly down the phone.

"Are you at the hospital?"

"No, he's in intensive care. They'll only let my Aunt in to sit with him, so I'm back at the clubhouse. I saw him earlier." Her sobs get louder. I can hear someone in the background comforting her.

"Do you want me to come over?" I offer.

"I don't think that's a good idea right now. The place is in uproar." She pauses to sniff. "Can I come sit with you for a bit?" She asks cautiously.

"Of course you can. You need me to pick you up?" I don't hesitate to invite her.

"No, it's okay. Eve will drop me off. I'll be there soon." She hangs up and I'm left staring at my phone.

I quickly ring Chris and fill him in on what's happened. I don't want Holly to overhear this conversation, and the sooner we can get control of this situation the better for everyone.

He's got some information for me, but doesn't want to share it over an unsecure phone line so I agree to drive to Melbourne tomorrow for a meeting with him. It's going to be a long journey there and back, but if I set off early enough it's doable.

When I've finished the call with Chris I go round my small apartment tidying things away before Holly gets here. It's not too bad, my military lifestyle means I normally pick up after myself, but running a bar often means I'm late to bed and early to rise and have started leaving things laying around in the interest of sleep.

Tidying up only took a few minutes and I find myself restlessly pacing the floor waiting for Holly to arrive. I keep checking my watch; surely she should be here by now. What if something's happened to her? I've just about decided to go searching for her when she walks in. She looks absolutely shattered.

I rush over to her, enveloping her in a tight hug. She feels so frail. She seems to notice our surroundings and looks around panicked for a moment. I know she doesn't want the club to know she's seeing me just yet, not with everything else that's going on. Luckily it's fairly quiet at this time of day, just a few regulars at the pool table in the far corner and they've not looked up from their game yet.

Josh is serving the bar and just gives me a nod when I ask him to keep an eye on things for me. I escort Holly upstairs to my apartment where she sinks into the sofa. When I get back from the kitchen with the coffees I've made she's shivering despite the heat of the day.

Placing the coffees on the table in front of us I sit down beside her, drawing her in close and placing a blanket over her bare legs. She's wearing cut off denim shorts and my cock is standing to attention, now's not the time though. Holly nestles closer into me, my arm protectively around her back and her head on my chest as she sobs quietly. I rub my hand soothingly up and down her back, so very different from the other night when my movements were slow and sensual. Today I just need to calm her, to hold her and to let her know she's not alone.

Soon she's breathing lightly, she's fallen asleep on me. This feels good, holding her while she sleeps. I lean back into the sofa, making sure that she's still comfortable and keeping her close. She sleeps for several hours, watching her sleep makes me drowsy, but I stay awake for her, maintaining my vigil, watching over her to make sure she's safe.

She wakes with a start and looks around her, unsure of her surroundings. It's the first time she's been in my apartment. She nestles into me with a sigh once she's reassured herself where she is and who she's with.

When she looks up at me with those dark eyes of hers I can't stop myself from leaning across and kissing her. She kisses me back. We make out on the sofa for a little while before she stops me. Standing from the sofa she reaches her hand out to me, pulling me up. From the way she's looking around my apartment I'm guessing she's looking for the bedroom. I nod my head to the door on the opposite side of the room and she pulls me along behind her until we're in my room. Holly pushes the door closed behind us and leads me to the bed.

As much as I want to take things slowly with her, especially when she's in such a fragile state I can't stop her when she starts to undress me. I'm hoping that she needs this as much as I do right now, because I don't think I can stop what's about to happen between us.

Holly and I spend the rest of the night discovering each other's bodies, sating ourselves with orgasms and ignoring sleep. I'm going to be so knackered come the morning, but it's going to be so worth it.

CHAPTER TWENTY SEVEN

HOLLY

I don't recognise the bed I'm in when I wake, but I do know the feel of the body that has me wrapped in its warm embrace.

I smile as I allow the memories of last night to come back. The sex was amazing. I'm surprised by how refreshed I feel considering the lack of sleep that we had. Then again, I do seem to recall falling asleep on Declan on the sofa not long after I arrived.

I'm not sure what woke me, when I hear the noise again. It's a quiet beep of an alarm. I strain to see the time on the clock at the side of the bed and groan when it's only 6am.

"I'm sorry." I hear Declan apologise. "I didn't mean to wake you." He leans over and kisses me gently. "I've got to go to Melbourne for a meeting this morning and needed the early start."

DECLAN

Holly looks at me in shock. "You're driving to Melbourne? But that's a five hour drive!" She exclaims. "When will you be back?"

"I'm hoping to get there, have this meeting and come straight back." I offer. "I can't cancel the meeting, it's too important. I'm sorry." Right now the last thing I want is a five-hour ride on the bike, but Chris has information he can only share face to face so I don't have a choice. I'd much rather spend the day in bed with Holly and tell her so.

"I'd rather spend the day in bed with you too." She grins. "I should go to the hospital I guess, sit with my Aunt for a bit."

While we're talking she's been checking her phone. She looks up at me. "No news is good news, right?"
What do I tell her? No news is sometimes bad news. I don't want to take the smile from her face though.

"Yep, if there was bad news you'd have heard by now. Cowboy says your Uncle's a fighter. I'm sure he'll pull through."

"Will you be back for the funeral?" I don't understand what she's asking me for a moment, her Uncle's still in intensive care. She sees the confusion on my face. "Scalp's funeral." She explains. "He was the president of Carnal MC that died. It's tomorrow."

"That's a bit quick isn't it?" I'm used to the long drawn out delay of military funerals.

"Maggie his wife wanted it done quickly. All his family are here so there was no reason to delay and prolong her grief." I'm about to say I didn't know the man when she stops me. "I know what you're going to say, you didn't know him. But I'd like you to be there for me." She gives me a small smile. "If you can. It doesn't matter if you can't get back though. I understand."

The chances of me making it back for the funeral are slim. I've barely slept and have a long ride ahead of me. I'd have to turn straight back round when I get to Melbourne to have any chance of getting back here in time.

"I'll try." I promise her. We both know it's probably an empty promise though.

HOLLY
Declan insisted on making sure I made it back to the clubhouse, delaying the start of his journey. I'm being

unrealistic hoping that he'll make it back for Scalp's funeral, and selfish. I just know that if he's beside me it will be a lot easier to handle.

I can't help but think back to the last funeral. Watching those two coffins beside each other in the church almost broke me. As sad as any funeral is, tomorrow is going to be a lot worse because of the memories it will bring back.

When I step back in the clubhouse Eve is waiting for me. The guys haven't noticed I've been gone all night but she has.

"Were you with him?" She asks quietly, careful not to draw attention to us.

I nod. She pulls me into a hug. "I'm glad you weren't alone."

"Is there any news from the hospital?" I ask. I'm starting to feel guilty for spending the night with Declan when I should have been here.

"No change." Eve looks sad. "But no news is good news, right?"

"No news is good news." I repeat, smiling wanly back at her.

With our arms wrapped around each other we head off to the kitchen to make a start on breakfast for everyone.

CHAPTER TWENTY EIGHT

DECLAN

It's late afternoon by the time I reach Chris's office in Melbourne. I ache everywhere, and I'm tired, so very tired.

Chris greets me warmly as he ushers me into his office. The private sector obviously pays well as it's lushly appointed, all highly polished mahogany and leather upholstery.

I'm grateful when Chris suggests we sit on one of the sofas at the back of the room, and his secretary brings us some freshly brewed coffee.

"How are you doing, Declan?" Chris asks. "I heard about Max, I'm sorry." He sounds genuine, not just the platitudes people come out with when they hear you've lost someone close to you. Chris met Max on a couple of occasions, I think they might have been poker games if memory serves, and I also think that Chris might have been on the losing end of Max's lucky streak.

"I'm okay." I shrug. "I'm getting too old for all this shit." I'm not thirty yet, so why do I feel so old?

"It's a different pace out in civilian life." Chris tells me. "It takes some getting used to, but you'll get there."

"I look forward to it." I take a welcome mouthful of the hot coffee, savouring it. It's just what I needed.

We spend a few minutes talking about mutual acquaintances and the state of the economy before Chris brings us back on track.

"What the hell have you landed yourself in the middle of Declan? This is some serious shit."

"I was hoping you could tell me." I laugh, but there's not much humour in it. It's more to try and defuse the tension that is building in the room.

"How did you end up in Severed anyway? Last I heard you lived in Perth?" I fill Chris in on my road trip with Cam and my impulsive decision to buy the pub.

"I loved it because it seemed such a peaceful place." I say ruefully.

"You landed in the middle of a disaster zone." Chris is serious now. "From what I can gather this is a new gang that's trying to establish a name for themselves on the drug scene. They're well financed, well armed and they're starting out in the smaller towns and looking to build up the trade until they're in a strong enough position to take on the big guys in Melbourne."

"Where's the money coming from?" I want to know who's backing this shit.

"They're pretty much self financed through a protection racket, but I think they may have recently got some additional funding and firepower from one of the South American dealers."

That's not good news. If the South Americans are involved then it's going to get dirty, violent and deadly that's for sure.

"Shit. Why couldn't I have bought a pub in a quiet little town?" I shrug.

"Because trouble follows you old man." Chris smiles and passes over a file. "What's in here can't leave this office, I'm not even supposed to be showing you it."

I scan the contents of the file. There are photos of the main gang members in there along with their criminal histories. They've all progressed from petty street crime to harder stuff, most of them have done time, but not as much as they should have which tells me that they've got a good lawyer on their side.

"They've not done much time between them have they?" I show Chris the sheet showing time served.

"No. That tells me they're unlikely to do much time even if we catch them red handed. Someone somewhere is getting paid too much money to keep them out of jail." Chris shrugs his shoulders in defeat.

We've been here before. This is the sort of situation we're used to going in and dealing with, covertly. We've seen some shit in our time, and not of our successful missions have been acknowledged, as we shouldn't have been there in the first place.

"We're going to have to deal with this ourselves, aren't we?" I look over the information in front of me, mentally calculating the manpower and resources that I'm going to need, and working out how many favours I can call in to accomplish it.

"I haven't got the manpower to spare right now." Chris apologises. "But I have got the firepower. I'll happily lend you that."

We need to know more information before we can come up with a strategy, the most important being the location. We also need to work out how far up the chain we need to go to ensure that this problem doesn't come back to Severed.

We discuss several scenarios, but until we have that last bit of Intel it's all theory and speculation.

It's the early hours of the morning before we put the file away back in Chris's safe. I'm not allowed to take copies of anything that I've seen so we've made sure I've memorised the important facts and faces.

Chris insists that I go back to his place and crash in his spare room. Crash seems to be an appropriate word, as no sooner has my head hit the pillow than I'm asleep.

Sleep isn't my friend this evening though. I've barely slept a few hours when Chris is shaking me awake.

"Fucking hell, Declan." He looks white. "That was some fucking nightmare." Chris tells me he heard my screams from the other side of his apartment. He also shows me the marks on his neck where I tried to strangle him when he came to wake me.

Shit. I can't do this. I realise that I can't sleep with Holly again in case I hurt her. The two nights I've been with her have been nightmare free, as has most of my time in Severed. It's not a risk I dare take though. I can't hurt this girl, she's becoming too important to me.

How the hell am I going to explain that to her?

Chris leaves the door into the hallway open so he can hear me if I cry out again. He doesn't need to. After the nightmare I just woke from I can't get back to sleep. I can't remember what it was about, just the feeling of terror followed by knowing I had to kill the person in front of me. It was them or me; life or death.

I'm a fucking ex special military soldier and I'm scared of sleep. Instead I lay awake and stare at the ceiling for the rest of the night.

I've got to get over this shit. War is about to descend on Severed and right now it looks like I'm the only hope they have.

We're fucked.

CHAPTER TWENTY NINE

DECLAN

We head back into the city to Chris's office; on the way he takes a detour to a warehouse that his company owns. When we get past the security at the gate and enter the building I let out a long breath. This place is like a military supermarket.

I look around at the crates of firepower, ammunition, tactical equipment and vehicles. It's like the set of some high action movie for fucks sake.

"What the fuck?" My jaw is literally hanging open; even in the military I never saw equipment of this quality in these quantities.

"What can I say?" Chris grins widely. "There's a lot more money in the private sector."

I look in a crate and pick up what I know to be the newest night vision goggles on the market. "But how?" I turn them over in my hand. "I didn't think these babies were even available yet?"

"I could tell you, but then I'd have to kill you." Chris smirks. He's always loved that cheesy line. "Seriously, I have excellent contacts and clients who expect the best of everything." His voice resonates pride when he talks.

"Chris?" I don't want to ask the question, but I need to know the answer now before I get in too deeply. "Just who do you work for?"

Chris could be affronted by my question; thankfully he's not. "You know I can't tell you that, Declan. What I can tell you is that I don't work for the bad guys. Right now, that's all I can say. I'm not helping you fight this little drug war of yours to benefit any of my clients. I need you to trust me on this."

I look Chris in the eyes and see the truth behind them. I let out a huge sigh of relief.

I'm still blown away by the stuff that Chris has in this warehouse. It's like a soldiers dream.

"Why did you bring me here?" I look around me, wishing I'd had some of this equipment back in Afghanistan.

"Because if you're going to take these guys on, you need to be prepared. I figure if you know what equipment I've got access to then you can write me a shopping list." Chris gestures at the crates surrounding us.

"I can't afford this stuff, Chris. I sank everything into the pub. Best I can manage is probably some combat rifles with the change I've got left in the bank."

"I don't want your money, Declan. I owe you. Consider this my way of repaying the debt." I blink in confusion, unsure how Chris thinks he owes me.

He sees my uncertainty and reminds me of a mission we were on together several years ago. I'd forgotten about it. Chris got caught behind enemy lines and I'd been the one they sent in to retrieve him. He sees it as saving his life from some bad ass motherfuckers; I just see it as another day on the job, nothing special.

"But..." I start.

"Shit, but nothing, Declan. Man, you saved my life that day. I consider it a debt, so do me a favour and let me repay you." He looks so earnest.

"Well, it would be rude not to I guess." I laugh.

"Great, have a look round then we'll head back to the office and write you up a shopping list." Chris gestures around the large warehouse.

I'm grinning wildly as I head off to inspect the contents of the nearest crates. I feel like a kid on Christmas morning!

CHAPTER THIRTY

DECLAN

I was like a kid in a candy shop rummaging around Chris's warehouse. I kept picking things up and just touching them to make sure they were real. Deadliest candy shop I've ever seen that's for sure.

One thing is clear, Chris has some considerable contacts. I don't know who he's working for, and perhaps I'm better off not knowing. I'm just glad to have him on side.

Chris's secretary brings us more freshly brewed coffee which is a good thing as my eyes are heavy from lack of sleep.

"You're lucky you're in Victoria and not New South Wales." Chris tells me as he delves into the plate of cookies that his secretary left on the desk between us.

"Why?" I ask around a mouthful of half eaten biscuit.

"Have you not heard of these new VLAD laws?" Chris looks surprised. "I thought you'd have been more on the ball."

"VLAD? What's that, I thought it was another name for Dracula." I laugh.

"I wish it was that funny. It stands for 'Vicious Lawless Association Disestablishment Act'. Basically they're cracking down on bikies. You need to be careful. If you're even seen talking to two or more patched bikers you can end up in prison."

I do a double take. I've never heard of the law, but it sounds extreme. "You what?"

The Government is trying to crack down on these outlaw bikie gangs. They're convinced that they're some sort of criminal kingpins and they're using these anti terrorism laws to stop them. Hell, there's a part of New South Wales where the Hell's Angels can't even visit their own clubhouse without being arrested.

"So I can be arrested for just talking to a couple of bikers?" I ask in disbelief.

"Yep, if one of them has a criminal record, even if you're unaware of it, then you can be charged with conspiracy to commit an offence."

"Fuck!" I can't believe what I'm hearing. The more Chris tells me the more outrageous it sounds.

"What the hell happened to democracy and being innocent until proven guilty?" I ask.

"Welcome to Australia." Chris laughs, but it's not a humorous, it's sarcastic.

"Just be careful. You need to keep an eye on this. From what you've told me a large part of your pub customers are involved with the MC in one way or another. If these laws become more extreme in Victoria, and I'm sure they will, then this is going to affect your business. "

"But these guys aren't criminals." I protest. "They're just a bunch of guys who love the lifestyle and live together. Shit, even their businesses are all legit." I protest.

"It won't make any difference." Chris sighs. "Anyway, let's not worry about what might happen and concentrate on what we need to do to get you out of this present mess." He brings the conversation back to the drug problem.

"I've got some contacts in South America." I raise my eyebrows when he says this. "Declan, I told you. I don't work for the drug cartels, but I do have contacts in them. You know that knowledge is currency in this business. Anyway, they've confirmed that the guys bothering you in Severed and new to the game. If we stamp down hard on them now no ones going to be shedding any tears over them."

"What do you suggest?" This is definitely in our favour. The last thing we needed was to find out the dealers had connections with some of the Mexican cartels. That's a war we definitely aren't equipped to win.

I've had some surveillance on the leaders, we're just waiting for them to lead us to where they're storing the drugs and then we can strike." Chris passes over some more photos.

The scary thing is that these so-called drug barons look just like you or me. You could pass them in the street and never know them for the death mongers' that they are.

Drugs are slow killers. They get you hooked with a few pills that make you happy, give you a temporary high, then they introduce you to the stronger stuff. The stuff you'd sell your soul for or that you'd steal from your mother for. Drugs don't just destroy the life of the addict; it's much more far reaching than that. They destroy the lives of the people who love you, the people you steal from to fund your addiction, and the people you introduce to them.

"What do you mean we?" I don't miss the way Chris phrased his last comment. "I didn't think you could spare any manpower?"

"I miss being out in the field sometimes." Chris looks at me. "Every so often I feel the need to get my hands dirty. I figure now is as good a time as any to go out and freshen up on my skills." Chris is grinning.

"Realistically, how many do you think we'll need? We don't know the size of the storage unit yet do we?" I question.

We sit and discuss the logistics of several theoretical situations. Between us we think we can get away with five trained personnel, calling on the MC for some additional firepower if needed.

"This MC worries me." Chris voices his concern. "They're an unknown variable. I don't like working with unknowns. They're dangerous."

"These guys have been through some serious shit this past few months. They can handle themselves. The guy I've been talking to, Angel, seems pretty calm headed, not one to rush into anything. They've got a personal stake in this, we either include them in the plan or keep a tight rein on them, or they'll go renegade and handle it themselves. I'd rather we worked together than at opposites."

Chris mulls the situation over. With Chris on our side we'll need three more trained personnel and I know just the men to call on. I'm just hoping they'll be able to come through for me. They've left the military behind and are getting on with civilian lives now.

Chris hands me the phone. "Call Cam. Tell him what's happening and ask him to speak to the guys. Don't worry about the logistics, I'll get them here."

I pick up the phone, hesitating to dial. I know we promised to always be there for each other after Max died, but what if they won't or can't.

There's only one way to find out. I tap out Cam's number and listen to it ringing at the other end.

"Hey, Cam." I say when he picks up. "I've got myself into a bit of a pickle and could use your help."

"What the fuck have you done now, Declan?" He laughs down the line at me.

"You'd better sit down mate, it's going to be a long story."

CHAPTER THIRTY ONE

HOLLY

The funeral was awful. It was always going to be, but it was made worse by some of the guys from Scalp's own club coming to blows at the graveside.

What the fuck is it with bikers? They always have to be so alpha male and fight for everything. Don't get me wrong I love the guys at Severed, but sometimes this whole lifestyle makes me feel suffocated.

Declan didn't make it back in time and I haven't heard from him. I sent him a text earlier asking if he was okay, but he hasn't replied.

I feel lost, like I'm trapped between two worlds, two lifestyles and I have to choose. I don't want to choose. Surely there's some hybrid option, some way to live in both, but I can't see it.

The club won't accept me seeing someone from the outside, and I can't see anyone from the outside understanding club dynamics. I'm not sure Declan would understand the pull of the club. It's more than family; I have a loyalty to the club.

I have a love/hate relationship with Severed. Whilst they are my family and I do feel they're looking out for me, I can't help blaming them for my losing Justice and Danni. If it hadn't been for the club none of that shit would have happened and my brother and best friend wouldn't be dead.

There are days when I don't know whether to run as far away from here as I can, and days like today where I can't imagine being anywhere else.

I'm not the only one that stood at that graveside today and remembered burying Justice and Danni. I could see it in so many faces. These guys have been to too many funerals lately. Cowboy held me close when it got too much for me.

Lucy has been sitting with me, trying to get me to tell wild tales of childhood adventures with Justice. I know what they're doing; it's good to remember the good times, especially on a day like this.

I don't want it to be Lucy sitting here beside me though. I want Declan. I'm being childish and selfish, but I can't help it. I check my phone again. Still nothing.

CHAPTER THIRTY TWO

DECLAN

The journey back to Severed was a lot more comfortable than the outward one. By the time we'd finished brainstorming in Chris's office it was past midnight. The tired bags under my eyes weren't the only give away; my whole body was sagging from exhaustion.

Chris informed me in no uncertain terms that he was sending me back with a driver. I'd refused another night in his spare room, needing to be back in Severed. My bike was securely strapped into the back of the large truck that was also packed ceiling high with supplies. War was definitely coming to Severed judging by the arsenal Chris was sending me home with.

Chris was staying behind to make the arrangements for Cam and the guys to join us. He'd follow on with them when they arrived in Melbourne.

There'd been no hesitation from any of the guys at coming out to support me. I don't know why I'd been so worried. They'd always had my back out on the battlefield and to them this was no different.

The relief when Cam had rung back to say they were all on board was indescribable.

We arrived back in Severed at dawn. The town was deserted and I was grateful for that as I showed Chris's driver where to unpack the supplies. I locked the garage door, pocketing the key before getting on the bike and heading over to see the MC.

I know I should probably have slept first. I looked like the walking dead at best, but I'd dozed on and off on the journey back. Chris's driver accepted the offer of one of the guest rooms out back and I left him to sleep the journey off.

When I arrive at the clubhouse the prospect holds me at the gate while he announces my presence to Angel. I'm soon buzzed in and greeted by Angel, Ink and Cowboy.

Cowboy looks concerned at my haggard appearance, but I tell him I'm okay. I take in the clubhouse when I ask him if there's anywhere we can talk.

"Yeah, yeah. Not as posh as your place. I get it." Cowboy rolls his eyes at me as I take in the bar and the lounge area. It's not a bad set up at all. I'm surprised they bother leaving to come to my place if I'm honest when they have everything they need here.

Angel leads us to what he tells me is the presidents office where he offers me a welcome shot of whisky.

Everyone starts to talk at once, until Angel silences them just with a look. That's good to see, there's a hierarchy here and there's also respect for command.

I fill the guys in on my meeting in the city. I'm struggling to stay awake as I tell them that we not only think we know who's behind it, but we're also now pretty certain we know where they're storing the drugs.

Angel seems concerned that they'll be no match numbers wise for this adversary.

I'm careful how much I share with the club. I obviously tell them that I have the team we need to deal with this and that I've called in some favours. Between us, we can and will handle this situation. What I don't share with them is how I have the contacts or anything from my past.

"You're asking me to take a lot on trust." Angel sounds cautious.

"I know. Have I said or done anything to you guys that would make you doubt me?" I do understand their concerns; frankly I'd be worried if they hadn't expressed them.

When I tell them I've seen evidence that the drug gang blew up Carnal's clubhouse he throws a spanner in the works.

"We're going to have to involve Carnal in that case." He tells me about the infighting they've got going on over the leadership and I can see that none of the guys in this room look happy at the prospect. Neither am I. Carnal are an unknown element. I don't like working with unknown elements.

I agree to let Angel know when I have more definite information for them and make my excuses.

"I need to get back and get some sleep. It's been a long ass night."

Wearily I head out from the clubhouse. The fresh air outside helps wake me up a little.

When I get back to the bar Lucy is on shift. She gives me a look that tells me how bad I look.

"Yeah, I know. I look like shit." I sigh.

"I wasn't going to say that."

"But you were thinking it." I give her a look that says I know otherwise. She laughs.

I'm so tired I think I'll sleep all day so I make arrangements with Lucy for one of the other staff to lock up for me. I'm so tired I can't even remember the rota without questioning her. That's not like me at all.

I drag my tired body up the stairs to my apartment, I'm not sure I'll make it as far as my bed. Right now the sofa is probably as far as I'll make it.

When I get to my door I see it's ajar. What the fuck? Who's been in here? I'm pretty sure I locked it when I left.

Easing the door open slowly I make my way into the room, gun drawn.

I'm certainly not expecting the sight that awaits me.

CHAPTER THIRTY THREE

HOLLY

The door swings open and I almost scream when Declan enters the room, gun held in front of him and his head scanning like crazy.

"What the fuck?" He shouts. "I almost fucking shot you!" He looks awful. There are shadows under his eyes and his face is covered in stubble that looks at least a couple of days old.

"I'm... I'm sorry." I stammer out. "I just wanted to see you." I start to shake when I realize just how close I came to being shot as an intruder.

"How did you even get in here?" Declan sounds exhausted. "I'm sure I locked the door?" He's so tired he's questioning himself.

I hold up the credit card that I used to jimmy his door lock guiltily. "My brother might have taught me how to break and enter when we were younger." I confess.

"I almost shot you." He repeats, his hand shaking slightly as he finally lowers the gun.

"Well. I'm glad you didn't." I try and hide my nerves with false cheer. It doesn't quite work as even I can hear the tremor in my voice.

"I'm sorry." Declan apologizes. He really does look done in.

"Are you okay? You look dreadful." Way to go Holly I admonish myself. Knock a guy when he's down.

"I'm shattered. I need to sleep." He heads slowly across the room to his bedroom ignoring me. He pauses just before he opens the door. "Go home, Holly."

I feel like I've been slapped. There's no affection or emotion in his voice as he dismisses me. Fuck that. I'm not a child to be told to go home.

I hesitate before letting forth a tirade of abuse on him. He's exhausted; any fool can see that and this fool needs to understand that.

I ignore his words and follow him into the bedroom. Without speaking I help him undress and he slides naked beneath the covers. I quickly remove my clothes as well and jump in next to him.

"I can't, Holly." He sighs, turning his back on me. I don't understand. Just a couple of days ago we were enjoying hot sex together. What's going on here?

I ignore him again, instead spooning against his back and wrapping my arms around him. "Shh, Declan." I soothe. "Just sleep, I'll keep you safe."

My poor boy is so tired he falls asleep quickly without further protest. I lay behind him, gently tracing my hand across his chest. His breathing becomes heavier and soon I think he's in a deep sleep.

The peace is soon broken when it's obvious he's in the midst of a horrific nightmare. He's starting to thrash and toss in his sleep and crying out unintelligible words.

I'm fearful of waking him when he's like this so I hold him tighter, whispering in his ear that I'm here, that he's safe. I repeat this until he calms down and drifts back off to sleep.

I must nod off myself. I feel incredibly hot when I wake, and realize that it's the heat of another body next to mine. At some point we've swapped positions and Declan is now spooning against my back. His arm holds me tightly against him, but I can tell from the gentle wheeze he's making that he's still asleep.

I reach a hand behind me, lazily tracing patterns on his leg. It's enough to wake him, I almost feel guilty for disturbing his rest until I feel the hard length of his cock pressing into my back. Declan's not the only one awake apparently.

"I told you to go home." He whispers in my ear.

"I know. I ignored you." I whisper back.

"You're going to be a handful aren't you, Holly." He says. I can almost hear a hint of disappointment in his voice.

"What's wrong?" I ask, turning to face him. Something's changed between us and I'm not sure what it is.

"We can't do this, Holly." He gestures between us.

"What do you mean we can't do this?" I question. "Your cock seems to think we can." I point at his erection, which obviously missed the memo saying we couldn't have sex.

"I'm dangerous for you, Holly. I can't be with you." He pauses, wondering how much he can tell me. "I have nightmares, bad ones and I hurt people when I have nightmares." He looks broken now.

"I know you have nightmares." I tell him. "You had one earlier." He looks at me in surprise. His eyes travel up and down my body, inspecting me. His hand moves to touch my throat. "What are you looking for?"

"I... I hurt people in my nightmares. Why didn't I hurt you?" He sounds so confused right now.

"Because I held you from behind and comforted you until it passed." I tell him. "I hugged your nightmare away."

"Really?" His voice is laced with disbelief.

"Really." I reach over and kiss him on the nose. "Silly boy, you couldn't hurt me." The look on his face tells me he doesn't believe that.

Slowly I work my way down his chest, kissing, nipping and teasing him. When I get to his erection I can't help myself, I take him in my mouth. I love the sigh he makes when I do that. The little moans he makes as I move my tongue up and down his hard length excite me.

"Fuck me, Declan." I release his cock from my mouth in order to make my request, taking it into my hand and pumping slowly instead. His cock feels so hot and ready for me.

He looks torn. "Please?" I beg. That does it.

"Holly." He groans. "Turn over." I do as he asks and Declan takes me from behind. The position forces his cock deeper than ever and I gasp and groan in pleasure as he thrusts in and out of me.

Without warning he slaps my arse, no one's ever done that to me before, but it feels good. The sting is welcome and I swear I felt his cock harden even more when he slapped me. He slaps me again, on the other cheek this time and I'm right. His cock does get harder when he slaps me.

We rut like animals, this is wild sex and it's fucking amazing. I scream out my orgasm. I can sense that Declan is close, so I surprise him.

"I want you to come in my mouth." I tell him.

"Fuck, Holly!" He gasps. "Turn over." I've barely got him in my mouth before he's coming down my throat. I swallow the salty taste of him, lapping at his cock with my tongue, sucking every last drop from him.

His groan when he came is the most amazing sound. I love knowing that I did that.

"I think I'm going to fucking pass out." He says, leaning against the headboard and over me. "That was... fucking awesome." He stammers out.

His breathing is heavy, and we're both coated in a sheen of sweat. Sex with him is just amazing. I've never slept with anyone like Declan before.

"Dirty boy." I laugh at him, tracing my hand along his sweaty back. "You need a shower."

"I sure do." He smirks back at me. "Fancy joining me?"

"Well, it would be rude not to." I laugh. "I'll let you go warm it up first though." I grin at him as I pull the sheet around me, covering me from the cool air in the room.

Declan laughs. It's a great sound. I don't hear him laugh very often, I get the impression he has a lot of hidden demons, so when he does it's a beautiful sound.

He makes his way to the bathroom, and I can't help commenting on the view. "Lovely arse you've got there."

"Yep, and it's all yours." He shouts back from the bathroom door. "You joining me or not?"

I jump out of bed and follow him. Yummy. Shower sex here I come.

DECLAN

I can't get over how good it feels with Holly. I came back from Melbourne determined to push her away, and yet here she is back in my bed.

The sex was amazing; the chemistry between us is the best I've ever felt. She says she calmed me down from a nightmare. I try to recall anything that would prove her right. I wish it was true, but I'm still scared that I'm going to hurt her.

If we're to stand any chance together then I'm going to have to get help. I don't want to admit I've got a problem, but it's the only way I can see a future for me and Holly. I can't be with her while I'm like a ticking time bomb.

Showering with Holly is fun, I'd love to wake up and start the day like this every day. There's a lot of groping, fondling and washing each other down. There's no sex as I think she's drained me dry. I can't believe she asked me to come in her mouth like that. Fuck, that was one hell of an orgasm.

Holly's sat on the bed brushing her hair when my phone rings. It's Chris. She seems oblivious so I take his call in the other room.

Chris has found the location of the drug warehouse. We need to act quickly. I tell him that I'll arrange a meeting with the MC's and brief them.

Chris tells me that he and the guys will be here this evening. I offer to put them up in the empty guest rooms out back.

"I've not started refurbishing them yet, they're still pretty basic, but they're clean." I offer.

"Shit, Declan. They'll be bloody heaven compared to some of the places we've bunked over the years." Chris laughs. He's right. We have been in some pretty basic accommodations during our service.

We end the call with Chris telling me he's flying the guys in by private plane to a local airfield. He'll arrange transport to the pub, but they'll arrive after closing to help things remain discreet. That's fine by me.

I put the phone back on the table and see Holly standing in the bedroom doorway. Shit. How much of that did she hear? The expression on her face tells me it was more than I wanted her to know.

"What's happening, Declan?" She asks between gritted teeth.

"Nothing, I've just got some old friends coming to stay for a few days." She doesn't buy it.

"Why do you need to sit down with the MC's and brief them? Who are you? What are you?" She's firing the questions at me now faster than I can answer them. Not that I can answer them.

"I can't tell you." I plead with her to accept my answer.

"Can't or won't?" She demands.

"Both."

"Fuck, Declan. You're mixed up in some shit and you're going to get hurt. I can't do this. I can't lose someone I care about again." There are tears in her eyes now. I can't stand knowing that I'm causing her pain.

"I told you I couldn't do this, Holly. I can't be with you right now, it's not safe for me to be with you." I'm backing away from her all the time I'm talking.

Shit. I don't want to lose her, but I can't see any other option right now. It's not safe to be around me. I can't promise her that I won't get hurt. I can't even promise her that her friends won't get hurt. If that happens I know she'll hate me.

"You don't have to do this, Declan." She pleads. "You can choose. You can choose me." Her tears are getting heavier.

I turn my back on her; unable to say the words she wants to hear.

"Fuck you, Declan. It's your loss." She screeches at me as she slams out of my apartment, the door shaking on its hinges as she crashes it behind her.

I sit there looking at the closed door for too long. I just lost my chance to save any chance I had of a relationship with Holly.

Sighing I pick up the phone to call Angel. I might have lost Holly, but hopefully I can still save the people she cares about.

CHAPTER THIRTY FOUR

DECLAN

The meeting between the two MC's was held at the Severed clubhouse. It was strange being inside the inner sanctum of an MC. There were parts of it that felt reminiscent of an episode of Sons of Anarchy, even though as a club Severed couldn't be more different than the Sons.

The contrast between the two clubs is vast. Where I've always held respect for Severed and the guys there, the other club Carnal seems totally different. I get the impression these are more like the Sons than I'm comfortable with.

The meeting was small, just the main players in the room. There was a lot of resentment from Carnal that an outsider had been allowed in, and was giving them orders.

Angel did his best to convince them that I was an okay guy, but I could still sense the distrust when the meeting broke up.

Razor and Viper from Carnal worry me. They're quick tempered and angry. They're out for revenge and seem unconcerned about who gets hurt as collateral damage.

They're dangerous. They're also fighting amongst themselves over who's going to take over the reins at Carnal.

At one point I thought Viper was going to go out there on his own, all guns blazing but Razor managed to rein him in. Razor is holding onto the reins by the narrowest margin. As much as he distrusts me he knows that he needs the guys and me. Viper is a loose cannon. I'd be happier without either of them coming on the mission if I'm honest.

The two clubs agree that I'll supply the firepower and my team, and that they'll both only send limited number of men, I've tried to stress how dangerous inexperienced personnel will be, but I'm not sure they've fully grasped how serious and just how dangerous this is.

The meeting ends and the assault is planned for tomorrow evening. That gives my guys time to rest and plan.

We'll spend the day going over surveillance photos and getting prepped. We can do this with our hands tied behind our backs.

I just hope that the two MC's don't fuck it up and get us all killed.

CHAPTER THIRTY FIVE

DECLAN

It was good to see the guys again, I just wish in some ways it had been under better circumstances. It's bitter sweet knowing we're all only back in the room together because of this drug war I've landed smack in the middle of.

The guys are ribbing each other over silly little things, Luke still can't get Jacko to open up about his vet nurse and I sense that there's a story there. I make a mental note to do some digging when we get back from this op. If we get back from this op.

Jacko and Luke scouted out a command area for us and spent the afternoon getting the supplies we needed out there.

We're going in fairly light, side arms, rifles, grenades and knives for the most part. We're expecting most of the combat to be at close quarters and we're relying on the element of surprise.

The decision has been made that we'll go in and secure the building before we let the MC's get involved. It's safer for everyone this way. As much as we'd like to keep them out of it I know we can't. If we try to do that they'll just go in all guns blazing and we'll end up with a load of casualties and no winners.

Cam and Chris have been on surveillance. The building looks derelict, it's a clever cover, but there's just enough traffic and noise to give it away if you know what you're looking for. Thanks to Chris's Intel we know the key players will be here this evening. It's the perfect time to strike.

The weather is not being our friend this evening; the night sky is clear and bright leaving no shadows for us to hide in. I'd have been happier with cloud cover or even rain. We'll just have to make the best of what we've got.

The MC's arrive and they're noisy as fuck. Lucky for us it doesn't appear that the enemy has noticed them. I can't tell if they look impressed or overawed by the weapons that we hand them. I think it's a mixture of both.

"That's a big building to cover." Angel whispers. He's right. There's more than one floor and there are windows all around it.

"It's not as bad as it looks, our surveillance has shown that the upper floor is empty, we've only got the ground floor to worry about." I reassure him.

We've counted around thirty guards which means that we're massively outnumbered, but I'm confident that stealth will see the odds reversed.

I manage to persuade the MC's to let us go in and clear the perimeter and we'll let them know when we need them to join us. Viper's not happy about it, but the others soon convince him he has no choice.

Cam pointed out the trip wires and sensors to them. They're not equipped to deal with them without setting off an alarm. We are, it's that simple.

I can see the curiosity in the eyes of the MC members. They're burning with questions, now isn't the time or the place for them.

My team set off, shadows in the night. It doesn't take them long to secure the perimeter. We made the decision that there will be no live casualties. Even my experienced ear can't hear the sound of the approach, nor the throats being cut as each assailant is overpowered. So far, so good.

Once the exterior is cleared we lead the MC guys into the heart of the building. A few of the workers are huddled in one corner of the large room whilst Chris covers them with a gun. These guys aren't a real threat, but they're witnesses and they won't see the morning.

The huge white spotlights create no shadows in the room, there's no place to hide. The centre of the room is filled with long trestle tables where they're mixing the drugs. The equipment looks expensive. Chris was right, they're well funded.

In the centre of the room Cam has one of the leaders tied to a chair, a black bag over his head.

Cowboy and Angel are still taking it all in. I walk over to them and realise from their shocked appearance that I probably look a little scary right now. I'm covered in a mix of blood and dust.

"We've got it under control here. It might be better if you guys get out of here and let us finish it off" I whisper, indicating the guy in the chair. "Plausible deniability and all that." Cowboy looks like he wants to throw up.

"You sure?" Angel asks, relief in his voice.

They're about to agree when the loose canon arrives in the room.

"Not so fast." Viper interrupts. He heads for the guy strapped to the chair, asking if it's the one who ordered the hit on his clubhouse.

"One of them." I confirm.

Viper goes over and puts a bullet in the guy's head. "Fuck". I didn't see that coming. We hadn't finished questioning him.

Viper stands in front of the body, smirking. The idiot then gets his dick out and urinates all over the dead body.

"Amateurs." I mutter under my breath. I finally persuade the MC's to go home. I can't risk them fucking up any more of the operation. Whilst we're armed with guns they leave bullets, and bullets are evidence. I wanted to do as much of this as possible without using them other than as deterrents.

Viper looks pissed off when I won't let him take the drugs with him. We're destroying them. There's no way I'm letting this poison ruin anyone else's life.

The MC is just heading out when one of the drug gang rushes into the room shooting wildly. Fuck it all to hell. I thought we'd cleared that corridor. I react instinctively. One shot from me and he's down – permanently.

I hear Angel swear and turn round to see him holding Cowboy. Shit. He's been hit. Cowboy has passed out. Luckily it looks like the bullet went straight through, he should be okay, just sore for a few days.

I persuade Angel that they need to leave now. I'll deal with the rest of it. I let out a sigh of relief when they're gone.

Chris has gathered up the paperwork we were able to find, he'll take that back with him and scrutinise it.

He passes us a couple of handguns to deal with the workers we've got tied up in the corner. The guns are registered to one of the cartels and can't be traced back to us. With any luck there'll be enough evidence left when we've destroyed the place to make it look like a battle between rival dealers. It's a powerful enough cartel that it will encourage any other wannabes to stay the hell out of Severed. We hope.

The fuses are set on the dynamite we've set. All the loose ends are tied up apart from one. This one's personal for me. When they attacked one of the women from Severed they stole a ring from her. It belonged to her late husband. I search each of the bodies until I find it. It's jammed onto the fat bastards finger and wont come off. I make it come off, discarding the bloody stump of his finger on the floor beside his lifeless body.

Now I feel like we've finished our mission.

We watch from a safe distance as the warehouse goes up in flames, checking the ruins afterwards to make sure that none of the drugs have survived the fire.

It's dawn when we walk away from the wreckage.

CHAPTER THIRTY SIX

HOLLY

I don't know what happened last night, just that something big went down and they brought Cowboy back almost dead.

I know that Declan was involved. I just don't know if he's in the same state as Cowboy or not.

The pubs locked up tight when I arrive, and there's no sign of Declan or his friends he said were staying over. I sit on the back step waiting, hoping.

A black van pulls into the yard and a group of guys jump out, patting each other on the back and congratulating each other. They go quiet when they see me.

I don't see Declan; my heart halts as I search the camouflaged faces, seeking out those bright blue eyes. I can't see them.

The passenger door of the van closes noisily; it's the wrong side of the van for me to see who it is. I hold my breath as I wait to see who's going to walk around it.

"Declan!" I screech, running towards him. I inspect him with my eyes, up and down his body. Fuck, he looks hot in the black overalls he's wearing. Thankfully I can't see any damage, although he's covered in a mixture of blood, sweat and dust.

The guys look at Declan in surprise, especially when he dismisses them with a nod. "Later guys, debrief after breakfast." They leave without a word. Who are these guys?

Declan places his hand on my arm and almost drags me along beside him to the back door of the pub.

"What are you doing here?" He asks between gritted teeth. It's not the reaction I was hoping for, but it is the reaction I was expecting after our fight the other day.

"I needed to know you were okay." I whisper.

"I told you to stay away, Holly." He sighs. "You're not safe around me."

"I'm a grown woman, Declan." I snap. "I'm old enough to make my own decisions, to choose the company I keep."

I turn to face him, grabbing his head between my hands and pulling his face towards mine. I kiss him deeply. He resists for a moment and I think all is lost, and then he returns my kiss.

"Look at you, dirty boy." I smirk as I take a step back. "I think we need to get you in the shower."

Declan throws his head back and laughs. "Well, it would be rude not to." He agrees.

CHAPTER THIRTY SEVEN

DECLAN

After a hot and steamy reunion with Holly in the shower I joined the guys for breakfast. There were a few curious glances when Holly joined us.

"I'm pleased for you, Declan." Cam pats me on the back when he sees Holly taking more food over to the others. "That girl has put the smile back on your face." He grins.

He's right. Holly has put the smile back on my face. Just a few months ago I didn't think it would happen. I'm so grateful that I was wrong.

"She has, Cam. I'm just worried I'll hurt her." I confess.

"Why?" He queries. "The nightmares? Chris told me what happened at his place."

"Yeah. What if I hurt her?" Chris looks thoughtful.

"You've gotten over the first obstacle mate by realising something is wrong. You can get help. The Army has doctors who specialise in this kind of thing." Chris sits down at an empty table and gestures for me to sit beside him.

"I'll make an appointment." I promise him.

"So, are you staying here?" He looks around the empty bar. "You've done a great job with it."

"I don't know." I tell him. "Part of me wants to, but if I stay then that's admitting that there's a chance of a relationship with Holly. The other part of me says to get the hell out of Severed and never see her again, for her own safety."

Chris contemplates my words. "Only you can make that decision, Declan. I can't make it for you. I think she makes you happy, I like the Declan I see when she's around you, but only you know how you're feeling inside."

He's right. I'm the only one who can make this decision, although right now I wish someone would make it for me.

"Hey, lover." Holly calls, bringing fresh coffee over to our table. She sits herself on my knee and plants a kiss on my cheek.

"What's that for?" I ask.

"I'm just glad you're safe." She grins.

Holly has such a simple way of looking at life. All she wants is for her friends and family to be happy and safe. I wish I could be more like her.

I look around the bar, filled with my friends and realise that for the first time in ages I do feel happy.

I just wish I didn't also feel like a ticking time bomb.

CHAPTER THIRTY EIGHT

DECLAN

Chris and the guys stayed in Severed for a couple of days and it was like old times. We drank, we partied, we played poker and I lost.

It's been good to spend time with them. I'm going to miss them, but they've all got their own lives to lead away from here.

We've agreed that we're not going to lose touch with each other, and re-avowed that if anyone needs help he only has to make a call and the others will be there to support him.

As we're hoping that's not going to happen we've also agreed to a meet up in Melbourne in a few months time.

It's hard saying goodbye to Cam, as he's still the one that I feel closest to. If it weren't for him I wouldn't be in Severed.

"You do realise this is all your fault, Cam?" I tell him.

"What's my fault?" He asks, fake hurt in his voice.

"That I'm here in Severed. I'd never have heard of the place if it wasn't for you."

"Ah." He pats me on the back. "In that case I can also take credit for introducing you to Severed which means you met that hot girl of yours as well." He smirks. He's got me there. Living in Severed hasn't been all bad.

"You decided what you're doing yet?" He looks at the pub behind us. "You staying or going back to Harvey?"

Holly chooses that moment to walk up behind him to say goodbye. She hears the line about staying or going and the hurt in her face is clear when I can't answer either of them. Holly gives Cam a hug goodbye, but doesn't stay around.

I'm stuck between a rock and a hard place. I don't know where I belong, or where I should go.

As the van drives off to take the guys back to the airport I return to my apartment in the pub.

Sue's ring is sitting on the drainer in the kitchen. I've cleaned it up for her, but not had chance to return it yet.

I write a short note.

> Sue, I understand that this belongs to you and I wanted to return it. I know how much this means to you. I hope it brings you some peace. Your friend Declan x

I seal the ring in an envelope with a note and ask one of the bar staff to drop it off for me on their way home after their shift.

I've tied up the last of the loose ends here in Severed, now I just need to decide if I'm staying or leaving.

CHAPTER THIRTY NINE

HOLLY

This morning has been a whirlwind of emotions. I left Declan and his friends at the pub, my heart breaking at the thought that he could even consider leaving us.

I'm under no illusion that this is some great romance, but I did think that what we shared was special and deserved a chance to see where it leads. I guess I was mistaken, for him it was obviously nothing more than hot sex.

There was uproar when I returned. Teresa had gone into premature labour and I watched them deliver her baby on the clubhouse floor. Through her tears I managed to make out that it had been triggered when she heard that Prez had come out of his coma, he's going to be okay.

The baby looks fine and I managed a quick cuddle before the paramedics took him and his mother off to the hospital to be checked out.

It's nice to see something good happen at the club after all the heartache they've gone through recently. It looks like Cowboy has finally found someone as well. I'm so pleased for him and Lucy. He's suffered so much, and held it all in.

That suffering reminds me of Declan. Lucy's helping Cowboy get over his demons. I'm pretty sure if Declan gave me a chance I could help him get over his.

"Holly, you got a moment?" I turn to see Eve gesturing to me.

"Sure, Eve. What's up?" She looks like she's got a secret that she's busting to tell. I love how enthusiastic Eve can get, I'm so happy that she's part of the club. She's good for everyone here.

Eve's waving a piece of notepaper in front of me, teasing me with it.

"What's that?" I try to look at it, but she won't stop wafting it and I can't see what's written on it.

"Proof that you've found a good guy." She giggles.

I'm confused and reach for the paper, but she holds it out of my reach.

"Eve!" I laugh. "Give it up or I'm going to have to take it by force." I joke.

"That's better." She smiles, handing me the note. "I much prefer your happy face, you were looking far too serious there." She walks off pleased that she's achieved her goal.

I look at the paper in my hand, not quite understanding what it is. It's a note from Declan to Sue. I've heard about this. He found her stolen ring for her and returned it.

Eve's right. This is proof that I've found myself a good man. Now I just have to fight for him.

CHAPTER FORTY

HOLLY

All the way over to the pub I've been second-guessing myself.

What if Declan really doesn't want me? What will I do?

I pull the truck into the yard at the back of the pub and switch the engine off.

I'm about to get out when I spot Declan. He's coming out of the back door of the pub with his arms full of luggage. I watch as he goes over to the bike and packs his bags into the pannier.

I'm too late. He's made his decision and he's leaving me.

I sit back in the drivers seat and close my eyes, willing the tears to stay away. I can do this. I'm stronger than this I tell myself even as I feel the track of a tear on my cheek.

There's a tap on the drivers window and it startles me. It's Declan. He's standing there, looking serious. I wind the window down.

"Can we talk?" He asks.

I nod my head and wait for him to tell me that he's leaving.

"Outside the truck would be better." I nod my head and he opens the door for me, helping me step out. "Let's go for a walk."

Declan takes my arm and walks us past his packed up bike. I can't bring myself to look at it. It hurts too much. We walk around the front of the pub and onto the main street without speaking.

"Holly, I…"

"Declan, I.." Our words cut each other off. After the silence we've both chosen the same time to speak.

"You first." He tells me. Shit. I don't want to go first.

I can't look at Declan so I talk to the empty street in front of us.

"Look, Declan. I get it. You need to get away from here. I'd hoped that we might have a future together, but I understand. You've got to do what's right for you." I pause to draw in a deep breath. "Thank you for the time we've had together."

I feel Declan's hand grasp mine and he turns me to face him.

"Silly girl." He whispers, reaching in and kissing me on the nose. "You're my silly girl though." He smiles. "I'm not leaving you, Holly."

I look at him in disbelief. "What?"

"I'm not leaving you. I think there's something between us and I want to see where it goes." He leans in again to kiss me. "If that's what you want?" He suddenly looks unsure.

"But, your bike?" I bluster. "You're packing, you're leaving." I can't seem to get the words out.

"Yes, I'm packing." He smiles. "No, I'm not leaving. We're leaving. Together."

"I don't understand?" I look around the empty street as if it will give me the answers. It doesn't. I'm still none the wiser.

"I figured we needed a few days away from here. Just the two of us. I was packing for us."

I'm still standing in the street, my mouth opening and closing like a fish, no words coming out.

"Holly, would you come on a romantic escape with me?" He invites me. "Just you, me and a cabin in the middle of nowhere for a few days?"

Will I? Fuck yes I will. I realise that I haven't actually answered him. "I'd love to. Yes please. When? Where?" I'm still not making sense nor can I string together a complete sentence.

Declan explains he's booked a cabin for us, and that with Eve's help I'm all packed up and we're going now. Just the two of us.

"There's an awesome shower there as well, I checked. I'd love to share the shower with you." He smirks before kissing me.

"Well it would be rude not to." I reply before kissing him back.

EPILOGUE

DECLAN

I've made the right decision to stay with Holly. The past few days hidden away in our cabin has proved that.

We've finally shared the secrets that were haunting both of us, including my disastrous night with Georgia and my fear of hurting Holly. She took it pretty well.

I'm still having nightmares, but Holly seems able to bring me out of them by holding me and whispering to me. I've agreed to set up an appointment and get some treatment when we get home. I owe it to both of us.

I still won't tell Holly what happened the night that Cowboy got hurt, but she seems to understand that I did what had to be done.

We're optimistic about the future, and we know we're definitely compatible together in bed. It's worth pursuing that's for sure.

Holly comes out of the bathroom in yet another skimpy little negligee, this one's all black lace and transparent. I can see her hard nipples through the flimsy fabric. I must remember to send Eve a thank you gift for packing Holly's bag for her.

Holly's stalking her way across the room to me as though I'm the prey and she's the predator. I do love it when my girl takes charge. My cock's already hard and standing to attention awaiting her first command.

The trill of my phone breaks the quiet of the cabin and Holly pouts. "Don't answer it, we're busy."

I make the mistake of glancing at the screen instead of looking at Holly. It's Cam.

"I won't be a minute, babe. Let me just answer Cam and we'll get right back to it." Holly pouts and comes to sit on the end of the bed.

"Hey, Cam. What's up? You know your timing sucks big time right now?" I laugh.

"Declan." Cam sounds serious. "You know when we said we'd be there for each other if needed? You meant it right?"

"Of course I did Cam. What's wrong?" Holly looks up when she hears the concern in my voice.

"Declan, I need you." Cam's voice is cut off. I can hear shouting in the background and then the call cuts off, but not before I hear the sound of a gunshot.

What the fuck? I need to get to my friend now.

ACKNOWLEDGEMENTS.

Thank you to Mark, for putting the smile back on my face, and for supporting my writing, you encourage me always.

To Colette Goodchild, who started off as a reader and has become my very special friend. She's there for me when I'm at my lowest, and helps me through the doubt.

To Francessca of Francessca's Romance Reviews who not only organises all my last minute tours, but encourages me and supports me and tells me off as if she was my mother! I can't tell you how much difference you make to me lovely lady.

To Tracie Podger, my fellow author who seems to be as enthusiastic about Declan as my beta team. It's an honour to know you, you crazy lady.

Thank you as always to my amazing team of beta readers, I couldn't do this without you.

To my fantastic street team who promote me for the love of it, thank you.

To the bloggers who share my teasers, review my books and bring you my new releases – I couldn't do this without you.

And to the readers who enjoy my books – thank you for giving me a reason to keep doing what I love.

OTHER BOOKS BY AVA MANELLO

CO-AUTHORED WITH K.T. FISHER

Severed Angel (Severed MC #1)

Carnal Desire (Severed MC #2)

Severed Justice (Severed MC #3)

Carnal Persuasion (Severed MC #4)

AVA MANELLO

Strip Back (Naked Nights 0.5 Eric's Story)

Strip Teaser (Naked Nights 1)

The 'Non' Adventures of Alice the erotic author (a series of short stories)

ABOUT AVA MANELLO

I'm a passionate reader, blogger, publisher, and author. I love nothing more than helping other Indie authors publish their books - be that reviewing, beta reading, formatting or proofreading.

I love erotic suspense that's well written and engages the reader, and I love promoting the heck out of it over on my book blog http://www.kinkybookklub.co.uk

STALK AVA MANELLO

Facebook:
http://www.facebook.com/avamanello

Twitter:
@AvaManello

Goodreads:
https://www.goodreads.com/AvaManello

Website:
http://www.avamanello.co.uk

AGAINST ME - CEDAR TREE 3

By Freya Barker
Released April, 2015

Add to Goodreads: http://bit.ly/1DlrIc8

SYNOPSIS:

Patience has always been Caleb Whitetail's strength. Quiet and unassuming is what you see with the GFI investigator, but the blood boils hot right under the surface. He kept his distance for years only to see the woman who has held his attention almost lose her life not just once, but twice. He is done standing in the shadows.

Katie Acker, once a tough and athletic security specialist now struggles daily to walk. The closest to family she has are her colleagues at GFI. Especially the man who saved her life and always has her back. So when she unwittingly becomes the focus of a Mexican cartel, it's no big surprise she finds him right by her side.

With the combustive change in their deepening bond, Katie and Caleb do not see the oncoming danger - until it surrounds them.

Read on for a sneak-peek!

ABOUT FREYA

Freya Barker has always loved being creative. From an early age on she danced and sang, doodled, created, cooked, baked, quilted and crafted. Her latest creative outlets were influenced by an ever-present love for reading. First through blogging, then cover art and design, and finally writing.

Born and raised in the Netherlands, she packed her two toddlers, and eight suitcases filled with toys to move to Canada. No stranger to new beginnings, she thrives on them.

With the kids grown and out in the world, Freya is at the 'prime' of her life. The body might be a bit ramshackle, but the spirit is high and as adventurous as ever. Something you may see reflected here and there in some of her heroines.... none of who will likely be wilting flowers.

Freya craved reading about 'real' people, those who are perhaps less than perfect, but just as deserving of romance, hot monkey sex and some thrills and chills in their lives – So she decided to write about them.

FIND FREYA HERE -

Facebook: http://www.facebook.com/FreyaBarkerWriter
Twitter: @freya_barker
Web: http://www.freyabarker.com
Goodreads: http://www.goodreads.com/FreyaBarker

PROLOGUE

The first thing I notice when she walks into the room are her pale green eyes. It almost looks like they are lit from within.

"Hey Katie, meet Caleb. He'll be working with us on contract basis, same as you."

I hold out my hand and she slips in her smaller one. Soft - the feeling of her skin against mine causes an involuntary shiver up my spine, and I notice her sharp intake of breath. I try to get a read on her, but her eyes lower under my scrutiny. *Hmmm.* Interesting. The top of her head reaches my chin, and to my large frame, her entire body seems much smaller than my first impression of her.

"Good to meet you." Her voice has a smoky sound to it, a deeper pitch, a quality you wouldn't expect coming from the woman with a pixie face, flowing dark hair and those large expressive eyes. Despite her athletic build, she almost appears fragile to me.

"Same here."

Her eyes flick up to mine and then move to Gus, owner of Gus Flemming Investigations, and the man whose reputation finally convinced me to give in to his tenacious pursuit of my services.

I am a loner. I don't generally work with partners or under a boss. I like my independence and the freedom it provides me, but I haven't been able to resist the lure of working with the investigator who has one of the highest success rates in the state. It helps that the case he called me in on hits close to home. Literally. A child gone missing from the reservation I grew up on. I feel this one deep. I left the reservation under less than friendly circumstance. My fifteen year-old sister had died after a brutally short stint with cancer, leaving my family destroyed. My parents were never the same and both my brother and I carried the scars of our fucked up family life, on our souls, after she passed away.

Only seventeen at the time, almost eighteen, I was marked by the experience and pissed off at the world. I'm sure they were happy to see the back of me when I enlisted.

"I want you to work together on the disappearance of this twelve-year old. Stick your heads together and see what you can come up with. She's been gone for seventy-two hours and her family is frantic. Details are in the file."

Gus hands each of us a folder and his eyes linger on my hand, the one that still holds Katie's much smaller one. Reluctantly I let her go to grab the file Gus is holding out.

Great. My first partner, and it has to be this woman. When I look at her, my displeasure must have shown on my face, because her eyes are shooting fire. I can hear Gus chuckle, "Don't underestimate that tidy little package you see there, my friend. Katie has proven herself to be a great asset to my team when called upon."

"What the fuck, Gus? Tidy little package? Sexist much?" She punches him in the shoulder.

"Ah babe, you know I couldn't do without ya..." Gus throws his arm around her shoulder and smiles down.

The interaction between the two should have been a warning.

*****

"Get behind me," I hiss at Katie as she is trying to get ahead of me into the small shed.

We managed to get a lead on the girl from one of her friends in Shiprock. Or rather, Katie managed. She was amazing at pulling the information from the twelve-year old friend. The missing girl had been talking to a guy online who had filled her head with promises and lies, finally convincing her to meet in town. Her poor parents were drowning in self-recrimination for not keeping a closer eye on her internet activities. But we had a place to start and with the help of a young computer wiz kid Gus has working at the office, we managed to identify the guy. A local kid; only eighteen himself, had been talking to her online for the past two months. When we visit his home address, he's not there, but his mother is. She directs us to the small building at the back of this abandoned business that belongs to his dad.

"Don't fucking tell me what to do, Caleb." Katie hisses back, pushing ahead despite my caution. Following close behind her

I see some movement from the corner of my eye just as we step inside. I instinctively throw myself on Katie, taking her down with force. The bullet that explodes from the shaking gun that had been pointed at her finds its way, unobstructed, into the wall on our other side. I roll off Katie and come up with my own weapon ready in my hand, aiming at the figure in the corner. The acrid smell of urine hits my nose as the kid who is holed up there throws down the gun and wets his pants.

"Don't h-hurt me," he stutters, his hands stretched toward me with his palms out.

"Jesus..." I run my free hand through my hair, scanning the small space, while keep my gun trained on the kid. "You okay, Katie?"

"Fine." Comes the terse reply.

"Can you check on her?" I nod my head in the direction of a pile of bedding, hiding what appears to be a very scared young girl. I get up and make sure the gun is far away from the kid's reach before pushing him face-down on the ground and securing his hands with a zip tie. "Is she ok?" I hear Katie's soothing murmurs as she checks over the terrified little girl.

"You hurting anywhere, honey?"

"N-no, he didn't hurt me," a shaky little voice answers Katie's question. "He loves me."

Katie looks over at me with her eyebrows raised, and I feel the same shock and frustration she obviously does. Fucking internet romance gone bad. And I almost killed the kid. Christ, I need a drink.

By the time we get most of their story the sound of emergency vehicles is filling the yard, and I grab my charge by the arm and pull him up.

"Come on, Romeo. Time to face the music."

Katie follows close behind with her arm around the pretty young girl who is crying. "He didn't do anything wrong! We just wanted to be together."

"Sweetheart, he is an adult and you are a minor. That is wrong. Not only that, he tried to shoot us with a gun he stole from his father's locker. That is all kinds of wrong."

Katie only succeeds in making the girl cry harder.

With both kids taken care of and her parents on their way to the hospital where she will be checked out, Katie and I are left staring at each other.

"Look-"

"Listen up-" Katie interrupts, "I'm sorry."

I'm surprised; I was about to apologize to her for taking her down so hard. "What for?"

"I could've gotten us hurt. I was pissed and not focused on my surroundings."

"Well I was about to tell you sorry myself, for trying to order you around. Still trying to get used to this 'partner' thing."

She cracks a little smile and it does something to me. Even the brief minutes laying on top of her in the midst of chaos, I was fully aware of every curve of her body and the faint citrus smell of her in my nostrils.

"Want to go for a drink with me and discuss our partnership?"

Her eyes go wide and she is about to answer me when the slam of a car door and fast approaching footsteps draw our attention.

"Holy fuck, honey - you okay?" Gus wraps his arms around Katie and presses a kiss to the top of her head. Oh. So that's how it is.

I shake my head slightly and try to shake the unfamiliar burn of jealousy. Damn.

After a brief report to Gus, I make my excuses and am on my way to my car when Katie calls my name and I turn around. Trotting up to where I'm standing by my truck, she grabs onto my arm.

"Rain check?"

I look over to where Gus is standing, talking to one of the officers left on scene and contemplate my answer.

"You let me know when you're available and I might take you up on it."

A flash of guilt passes through her eyes and with ae walks back over to his side.